Praise for *A Stone's Throw*

"I love this book. Young Orvie takes you by the hand and none-too-gently pulls you right down into the lovely muck of his funny, mysterious, heart-breaking world."

—John Manderino, author of *The H-bomb and the Jesus Rock*

"Mort's writing is every bit as wonderful as the food in his splendid restaurant."

—J. Courtney Sullivan, the author of the *New York Times* best-selling novels *Commencement, Maine,* and *The Engagements*

"*A Stone's Throw* evokes rural postwar America through a series of spare, vivid, funny, unflinching vignettes. The power of these wonderfully simple tales snuck up on me."

—Lewis Robinson, award winning author of *Officer Friendly and Other Stories*

"The day-to-day musings of a boy in 1940s small town America, from the mundane to the profound, come to life in this charming series of vignettes."

—Dana Pearson, author and columnist

"Mort Mather has a gift for pulling us into Orvie's world so we can see shadows of ourselves beside him. The author's background in agriculture is evident in the delightful way he describes how Orvie deals with garden bugs, hay wagons, horses, damming up streams, and the discoveries and loneliness of rural life."

—David Morse author of *Harry and Maude Take It On*

"I like it better each time I read it—and I liked it a lot the first time around!"

—Marshall Burchard, author of numerous children's books and three time editor of *A Stone's Throw*

"Mort Mather has captured the feel, the sounds and smells of rural life in the 40's."

—U.S. Congresswoman Chellie Pingree

A
STONE'S THROW

Orvie's Stories

MORT MATHER

A STONE'S THROW
Orvie's Stories

Copyright ©2016 Mort Mather

ISBN: 978-1-63381-067-9

All rights reserved. Except for brief quotations used in reviews and critical articles, no part of this book may be used or reproduced in any form or by any means, electronic or mechanical, including photocopying, recording, or by an information storage and retrieval system, without permission from the author.

designed and produced by
Maine Authors Publishing
Rockland, Maine
www.maineauthorspublishing.com

Printed in the United States of America

Acknowledgments

I was trying to write something for *The Sun* magazine when I joined a writers group in Kennebunk started by David Morse. Several months in I wrote my first Orvie story. It was so well received by the group that I wrote another and then another, until five years later the group urged me to put them together in a book. Special thanks to David Morse, Celine Boyle, Celeste Dynan, Patricia Leavy, Ning Sullivan, and Steve Herhovcik. Patricia was also instrumental in getting one of Orvie's stories published in *On (Writing) Families* (Sense Publishers).

John Manderino, author of *Sam and his Brother Len* and three other critically acclaimed novels, was the first to read and provide editorial advice on the stories in an order I felt was a progression in Orvie's age. Lewis Robinson, author of *Officer Friendly*, edited/advised two rewrites. He saw it as a novel and suggested some additional chapters to fill it out. Karen Stathopolous and Marshall Burchard provided excellent editorial help.

Barbara Jones Mather, my wife of 46 years, has been my editor in chief since I began writing a weekly garden column in 1972. After her edits of my pencil-written columns I typed them with carbon paper copies on an old portable typewriter. A few years later she surprised me with the best Christmas present ever, a new Smith-Corona typewriter that, though replaced by computers, still holds a special place in my heart.

Contents

A STONE'S THROW

Orvie's Stories ▶

1955

Prologue

I feel the bus slow down and check my watch for the millionth time—midnight, the time it is due in Jacob Lake. The bus is dark; the few other passengers are probably asleep. I pick up my bag with the clothes I'll wear for the next couple of months and move to the front. It's dark everywhere except for the headlights—no house lights, no cars or trucks, just the road. Then the headlights pick up a building with a gas pump out front, and then the sign on the building: "Jacob Lake Trading Post." I see the Jeep, the same Jeep Dad drove away in when I was thirteen, never to come east again, he said. He gets out and comes toward me as the bus pulls away.

"You've grown quite a bit," he says as he takes my bag.

"Yep. I guess." What else should I say? So have you? You look good? How are you doing? We get in the Jeep, and he congratulates me on graduating from high school and asks how my trip has been. I tell him about the plane ride to Chicago and the bus to Flagstaff and spending the day walking around Flagstaff until it was time to board the bus to Salt Lake City. It all seems pretty boring. He tells me it will take about an hour on this dirt road we're on before we come to the turnoff for the fire-lookout tower he mans in the summer. There's a cabin at the base of the tower, he says, where we'll live until the first snow.

We don't really have much to say. It's awkward. I could tell him how I changed my name by registering for high school as "O. Charles" instead of "Orville" and how the teachers at roll call read my name as "O. Charles" and how the kids from school called me "O.C." and the kids who didn't know me from before called me "Charlie," but I don't. Maybe I did it because I was mad at him for leaving and didn't want to have his name anymore. I don't know. He might have asked me why and I didn't really have an answer.

What I want most is to get my parents back together. I'd never written anything like that in letters, but I thought about it a lot. I'm pretty sure Mom would come west if he asked her, and I'll be going into the Army in a couple of months, so I wouldn't be any bother.

"I think Mom still loves you." I hadn't intended to say that so soon, maybe not at all, but he wasn't saying anything. He still didn't say anything and then:

"Well, son, you'll meet your brother and sister when they get up in the morning, and Georgette, their mother, is waiting up for us."

A brother and a sister? The headlights bounce along the road ahead and reflect off the trees close by both sides. The letters I'd gotten over the past five years—not that many but still…a brother and a sister?

"Does Grandma know?"

"No. No one back east knows. You can spread the word or not, as you wish."

As I wish? Grandma doesn't even know? How did this happen? Who is Georgette?

"You have another wife?"

"Yes. I married Georgette in Reno after I divorced your mother."

4

So much for getting my parents back together. I guess Dad's passion for painting western landscapes was not the only reason he left my mother and me to never come east again, he'd said. He also left to be with someone he worked with in New York and when he drove away from our farm five years ago he headed for the train station to pick her up before turning west.

So here I am, a couple of thousand miles from home, riding through the night making small talk with a father who walked out on me, about to meet a step-mother I never knew I had, as well as their children, who are also news to me, my half-brother who is three and my half-sister who is eighteen months.

1942

Screen Door

"Mom, come here!" I holler from the bank by the road where I'm working.

"What is it, Orvie?"

"I want you to see something."

"I can't right now; I'm busy. Come here and tell me about it."

I run in from the city I been building with sticks and dandelion stems and leaves, but when I get to the kitchen door it won't open.

"Can I come in?"

"*May* I come in?"

"May I come in?

"Tell me from there, Orvie."

"Why can't I come in?"

"I just cleaned the floors and you're all dirty. I don't want you tracking in and out. Tell me from there."

"I made this neat thing. It's like a city with roads and bridges and tunnels. It even has running water."

"Running water? That *is* something. How did you do that?"

"Come on out and see!"

"I can't right now. I have things on the stove. Tell me about it."

"Well, you know that thing you have to take the cream off the milk? That glass tube?"

"Yes, the siphon."

"Yeah. Well, I made one out of dandelion stems. I put the small end of one into the big end of another and hooked up a whole bunch of them and made this pipeline down the bank. It doesn't go straight down but kinda curves around some things and ends up up in the air so you can see the water coming out of it. Then I got a bucket a water and put the top end in there and then I sucked on the bottom and the water started coming out. It's falling into a hole I made that will fill up and be like a swimming hole for people."

"Wow! That's quite inventive."

"Come see!"

"Not now. Now leave me alone for a bit."

"You don't love me anymore."

"Come on, Orvie, I've got to concentrate on what I'm doing."

"You do not."

"Do so."

"Do not."

"Do so."

"Do not, do not, do not, do not."

"Orville, if you don't leave me alone, I'm going to throw this glass of water at you."

"Will not."

"I'm warning you," she says as she fills a glass with water and sets it on the counter where I can see it.

"You won't because the clean floor will get wet, so there."

I fall down laughing, wet with the water she threw at me through the screen door. I really didn't think she would do it but she did. She laughs, too. I tease her some more until she says, "Orvie, seriously now, please go back to what you were doing and leave me alone for a little bit. I'll be out as soon as I finish what I'm doing."

"What are you doing?"

She stomps her foot and starts to fill the glass with water again. "Skedaddle!"

I skedaddle.

It turned out what she was doing was making a cake for me, which was a surprise 'cause I'd plumb forgot it was my birthday.

My Best Friend

Mom is standing at the bottom of the stairs instead of by the stove when I come down for breakfast. "Happy Birthday, Orvie. Let me give you a big hug."

Dad picks me up and hugs me too. "Happy Birthday, son; you're getting heavy." While he's holding me I notice a big box over near the fireplace.

"What's in the box?"

Dad puts me down. "Take a look."

I run over, and in the box is a little brown puppy. "Oh! Wow! Is he mine? What's his name?"

"That's up to you. He's your dog, so you should name him."

"He looks like a little bear cub. I'm going to call him Cubby."

"He won't be a little fur ball for long."

"He's licking my face. Oh gosh! He tickles! Thanks, Dad. Thanks, Mom."

I play with Cubby all the time. We are the best friends. I give him food and water. Dad opened up the box to make a pen for him in a corner of the kitchen, and we covered the floor with newspapers to make it easier to clean up his pee and poop until we get him house-broken. I can take him out of the box to play with him, but if he has an accident I have to clean it up. He has really sharp teeth, and sometimes when we are rolling around on the floor he bites me, but I can tell that if he hurts me he is sorry. If I say "Ow," he stops wrestling and kinda turns his head to the side a little and looks at me in a certain way, and I know he is saying, "Did I hurt you? I'm sorry." And then he licks the place he bit me to make it better.

A Stone's Throw

"**M**om, what's in that big pot on the stove?"

"Boiling water. Orvie, I wish you wouldn't let the screen door slam."

"Play with me."

"Not now, Orvie; I'm busy."

"Aw, come on. Come on down to the bridge and play Pooh sticks with me."

"I'm busy."

"You're always busy. Just one game."

"Go outside and play."

"I don't have anybody to play with. I wish we never came here."

"I thought you liked the farm."

"Yeah, I do, kinda, but there's nobody to play with. There wasn't many kids...."

"Weren't. There weren't many kids."

"There weren't many kids, except Kitty, but there's nobody here."

"You'll find some friends. It just takes time. You'll be going to school soon and you'll meet lots of kids."

"They won't live close. Nobody lives close here. I ain't seen any kids at all."

"Please don't use that word; it makes you sound igno-
rant."

"Why won't you play with me?"

"I told you I'm busy. Now leave me be."

"Whatcha doin'?"

"Canning beans. I've never done it before and I have to
concentrate, so leave me alone."

"Can I help?"

"No, you *may* not. The water's hot and it's messy. If you
want a job, sweep the floor."

I just go outside and sit on the steps for a while.

I'll kick this old stone down ta the bridge. Shucks, it went
off the road. Kick, kick; hard to kick it out of the weeds. There
it goes. Good one! Road is dusty down here. Think I'll drop the
stone into the brook.

Dad says this is a stream that flows into the brook that
runs through our farm, and I guess he's right, as this is so small
I can jump across it but the brook is too big to do that. There's a
place where the banks are low on both sides and the brook isn't
too deep to drive the Jeep across, which is what Dad says he will
do when he wants to mow the field on the other side, which is
pretty much a hill. He says he needs to mow it to keep it from
growing up in bushes and trees. He says we can go sledding on
the hill when it snows, and maybe the brook will freeze so we
can walk across.

Took me about twenty kicks to kick the stone from the
house to the bridge. I'm gonna run up to the house and see
how many throws it takes me. I'll start right at the corner of the
wood shed.

One. Good throw.

Two.

Three. I'm about halfway there.

Four. Where'd it go? There it is under that big leaf.

Five. Close enough. If I'd'a thrown on a straight line, I could'a done it in five. Course if I'd thrown it down the road, it'd prob'ly'a bounced most of the way.

"Mom!"

"Land sakes, Orvie, you startled me."

"Can you throw a stone from the house to the bridge?"

"I don't think so."

"Can Dad?"

"It's pretty far."

"I don't think he can, but he said the bridge was a stone's throw from the house. Why did he say that if it wasn't true?"

"Orvie, you slay me. That's just an expression people use to say that something is pretty close."

"Oh. So Dad wasn't lying?"

"No. Whoever he said that to would get an idea of approximately how far the bridge is from the house."

"Can you play with me now?"

"No, Orvie. Read a book."

I go back to the bridge an' play Pooh sticks by myself.

Big Black Lopsided Car

"**M**om, I hear a car."

There aren't many cars that come by, and I can tell every one of 'em by the sound. Mom can't. I'll tell her the Balichs are coming and when they drive by she'll be surprised that I was right. Whenever a car comes along, everybody stops to see who it is an' wave if it's a neighbor, which it usually is. She knows Mr. Crosby's sound because he comes every day with the mail. The road is mostly only wide enough for one car and everybody drives down the middle, but when two cars do meet they just go real slow while passing each other. Most often they go so slow they wind up stopping and talking for a bit.

The road grader comes by in the spring to smooth the road, but it don't really do all that much 'cept maybe make the road lower between the banks, least ways that's what my dad says. The road goes right through the middle of our farm; the house, wagon shed, and slate-roof building are on one side of the road, and we have three chicken houses and a big barn on the other side of the road. Everything's pretty close together, so when a car drives by they are only a few feet from most of our buildings—less than a stone's throw, even if I'm throwing.

I don't recognize the sound of this car, so I'm guessing it's Grandma King and Aunt Hattie—that's my Mom's mom and aunt who we are expecting. Mom is real excited 'cause she hasn't seen her mom since before we moved to the farm. Mom comes outta the kitchen wiping her hands on her apron just as the car comes across the bridge.

Mom's mom is little. I'm almost taller 'n she is and I'm only six years old. Her sister, Aunt Hattie, is huge. She must weigh a thousand pounds. When she gets in the car the car sinks down on her side. She doesn't drive but she owns the car, and Grandma drives wherever they go. Grandma needs lots of cushions to get her close to the wheel because they can't move the seat forward or else Aunt Hattie can't fit in. Mostly Aunt Hattie sits in the back insteada trying to squeeze into the front seat, but even so Grandma King needs cushions behind her. But she can't sit on cushions because her feet have to reach the pedals. She can't even see over the steering wheel, which looks kinda funny.

They're only gonna stay one night. Mom wishes they could stay longer, but they can't because Aunt Hattie wants to get back home. They're going to New York tomorrow to visit Mom's sister. It took 'em three days to drive from Pittsburgh. I heard Mom ask Grandma why Aunt Hattie came, as she didn't seem to be enjoying herself. Grandma said she really didn't know but when she'd asked Aunt Hat if she could borrow the car for the trip Aunt Hattie said she wanted to come along and what could she do since it was her car. It's the farthest Aunt Hattie has been away from home, and Grandma doesn't guess she'll ever want to do it again. She just sits in the middle of the sofa waiting to eat, which is also where she's going to sleep. She's not too good with stairs. Seems to like Mom's cooking OK, which I must say she'd have to be crazy not to because my mom is a really good cook.

Mr. Hitler

Mom is always in the kitchen stirring something on the stove, mixing something, or peeling potatoes or carrots or cutting up stuff. When she fills up the compost bucket, I have to take it out to the compost pile, and when she fills up the trash basket, I have to take it down by the stream and burn it.

"Mom, why are you taking the label off the can?"

"We can burn the paper in the trash, and Mr. Roosevelt says he wants all the tin he can get."

I wish he'd take the paper, too.

"Why does he need tin?"

"They need it for the war."

"Why are you taking out the bottom?"

"Well, I put the top and the bottom inside like this and … ." She puts it on the floor. "Here, step on it. Harder." I stomp on it and jump up and down 'til it's flat as a pancake. "That's it. Now that it's flat it takes up less space. When I get this bag full, we'll take it to the community house and they'll put it in a truck and take it someplace where they can melt it down."

"Why?"

"We all have to do our part to save the world from Mr. Hitler and the Japs. The tin will go to make more ships and planes. Did you see the picture your Dad is working on?"

"With the face of a sailor and a soldier and smoke and fire and airplanes behind them?"

"Yes. The words say, 'Buy Bonds. Support Our Boys Overseas.' Everybody has to do what they can to help the war effort."

"What are bonds?"

"It's like a loan."

"Do we have bonds?"

"Actually, you do."

"I do?"

"Grandma and Grandpa gave you a bond for your birthday last year."

"How much money will I get?"

"Twenty-five dollars."

"Wow! Are Grandma and Grandpa rich?"

"You kill me! No, not at all. They only had to give the government about half that much; the rest will be interest."

"So the government's rich."

"That's an even bigger laugh."

Rainy Day

I like being outside more'n being inside 'cause there's more to do. Can't play ball in the house. I don't feel like reading. I was just playing with Cubby but Mom told us to stop roughhousing. I asked her if we could make cookies or something but she's too busy an' told me to read something.

It's not raining that hard really. Whenever I see rain like this I remember the time I was waiting for Dad to come home from work when we lived near the city. He always came home at the same time and Mom would tell me to go look for him and I would go sit in the window and see him coming down the street, but this time he just came in the door before I thought he would but the biggest surprise was that he wasn't wet because it was raining cats and dogs. When I asked him how he got home without getting wet he told me he ran between the raindrops. I think that was really pretty amazing, 'cause whenever I try to run between the raindrops even when it's not raining very hard, I can never do it.

I tell Mom I want to go to the barn to play and she says I'll get wet and I tell her I'll run between the raindrops and she laughs and thinks that's pretty funny, but I tell her if Dad can do it, so can I. She asks where I ever got such a notion that he could dodge raindrops, and I remind her of when he came home from work and wasn't wet and she told me he took a taxi. What a dummy I was for believing that!

Christopher Robin watched raindrops run down the window and would choose a drop to win the race. It's really pretty interesting because I might think that I got a good fat raindrop that's sure to win and then two other small drops get together and zip, they're gone, or a drop from the sky will hit a smaller drop and zip again—I lose the race. But watching raindrops run down the window is still about the most exciting thing I can do when it's raining.

Christopher Robin invented "Pooh Sticks," which I like to play myself. Ya drop two sticks or leaves or whatever will float into the stream on one side of the bridge and then run over to the other side to see which stick comes through first. It's more fun if two or three people do it, but I just pretend that one stick is mine and the other one is somebody else's. Sometimes only one will come through and I go under the bridge to see what happened, like a shipwreck or something. There's a place where the water just kinda goes around and around and the stick will be there just going round and around, but I know where to drop the sticks so they don't get stuck in that place, but other times they get stuck on the side of the stream like the crew on the ship had to go ashore to take a leak or something.

"Mom, can I have a blanket?"

"*May* I have a blanket?"

"May I have a blanket?"

"If you're cold, go put on a sweater."

"I'm not cold. I wanna make a tent."

"You may take the blanket that's folded on the foot of my bed."

"Thanks!"

The sofa is a good place to make a tent. I just throw one side of the blanket over the back of the sofa and the rest of the blanket over the front of the sofa and crawl in. It's really fun, like having my own house.

"Mom, can I have a flashlight?"

She just looks at me.

"May I have a flashlight?"

"You know where they are."

I need the flashlight because it's too dark in the tent to read. I don't really wanna read, though, so I stash the flashlight and the book behind a cushion and just lie there for a while. What I need is a bigger tent. I got a idea! Oh, this is going to be swell. I take off the blanket and turn up the cushions at the ends of the sofa and put two cushions on end beside the little table in front of the sofa and then put the blanket over. This is even better than I thought. Now I have a front door. I crawl under the table and up between the table and the sofa and I'm home! I mean really home, my own house that I made all by myself.

If I had a girlfriend, we could play house. We could pretend I went to work and when I came home she would kiss me and fix me a drink like Mom does for Dad and then we would have dinner and maybe read a while or listen to the radio and then go to bed. That would be nice, just lying here next to each other, maybe our legs touching.

If Cubby got in here, he'd mess it all up. Even if he was calm and just lay here next to me, he'd wag his tail and mess it up.

One time when we had company I hid in the sofa. I know grownups talk about different stuff when I'm not around, so if they don't think I'm here I might learn some interesting stuff. I squeezed myself down behind the sitting cushions and then hid myself with the back cushions. I was so small I disappeared. When the grownups came into the living room they looked around and couldn't find me.

"Where's Orvie?" they said. "I wonder where he could have gotten to." And other things like that. They even sat on the sofa and didn't notice that I was there. I stayed hidden and spied on them listening to what they were saying until Mom served dessert. The most interesting thing they said was that they would get more dessert because they could have mine. That's when I showed them *that* wasn't going to happen.

Old Picture

We have two attics. Dad says that the part of the house that is the kitchen wasn't built when the rest of the house was built, which is why we can't get from the bedrooms on one side to the bedrooms on the other side without going downstairs. He says that someday he plans to knock a hole through between the two upstairs so we don't have to go downstairs and upstairs just to get to the spare bedrooms, but it would be hard to get through all the stones in the wall, which is pretty thick. There is a window in the attic that connects the two attics, which Dad says was a window when the first part of the house was built, and he says the stone wall he will have to break through will be thicker than where the window is because the walls are thinner at the top than the bottom. I guess because they didn't want to lift the bigger stones up so high.

In our attic there's a big trunk that's taller than I am, and it is full of Mom's old clothes, which are nothing like what she wears now. There's a dress that's real smooth that I like to feel, even though it smells of mothballs. Beside the trunk is a big box with stuff from the World's Fair which Mom and Dad went to. My favorite souvenir is a neat little box with a door that when you open the door there is white furry stuff that Mom told me is spun glass.

In another trunk there are lots of pictures and letters and cards and some little books with little pencils that Mom says were for when she went to dances. The boys would ask her for a dance, and if she wanted to dance with them she would put their name in the little book for one of the dances. I found a picture of an old car with flags draped over it, the top down, and a pretty girl and a boy dressed up like American flags riding in the back seat, waving to a crowd of people along the road.

"Mom, who's this?"

"For goodness sakes, where'd you get that?"

"In the trunk in the attic; who's the girl?"

"That's me."

"That's you?"

"Yep, when I was about your age."

"What are you wearing and who's the boy with the beard? Was he your boyfriend?"

"No, Bobby was younger than I was. We were dressed up as Uncle Sam and Miss Liberty for the Fourth of July parade."

"What's the sign say?"

"Sound it out."

"P ... E ... A ... C ... E."

"Umhum."

"Pee-a-see ... peace!"

"Good."

"Peace with haw...."

"The H is silent."

"Peace with on-or."

"Good. Peace with honor, firm...."

"... ness. Firmness!"

"Right."

"Pr…os…per…i…. Pros…per…it…y. Prosperity?"

"Excellent!"

"Peace with honor, firmness, prosperity. What's that mean?"

"Well, there was a war going on in Europe and Mexico, and everybody was afraid the United States might get into it. President Wilson was up for reelection, and he told everybody they should vote for him because he kept us out of war, which is why he said 'peace with honor,' and firmness is just a good quality for a president to have, and all politicians are for prosperity."

"That's a really old car. Did Mr. Wilson drive the car?"

"Don't make me laugh! No, Bobby's father drove it. It was his car and it was a pretty new car at the time, a Model T Ford, real spiffy. Bobby's father and my dad were both lawyers and were friends most of the time, except when they got into politics. I think Mr. Johnson asked me to be in the parade for the Democrats just to get my father's goat. And I must say my dad got real mad and wasn't going to let me do it, but my mom got him to change his mind. I asked her how she did it, because my dad was really, really mad, and my mom just kind of smiled and said she had her ways."

"Did Mr. Wilson win?"

"He did."

"Did that make your dad mad?"

"You bet, and then President Wilson got us right into the war. It was the biggest war ever; millions of people were killed and your grandfather got to say, 'I told you so.' But that didn't really make him happy."

"You were real pretty, Mom."

"Thank you, Orvie."

Teasing Blood Suckers

Cubby is getting big just like Dad said he would. We like to hang out on the stream bank watching the water go by and checking out the fish. There aren't very big fish. Big fish wouldn't fit in this little stream. Just minnows. If I put my foot in the water, pretty soon a blood sucker will come humping along. I don't know how they know my foot is there, but it don't take long for 'em to find me. They don't swim like a fish. They just kind of get smaller and larger, but whatever way they do it they can move. Just as they get to me I pull my foot out and watch 'em swim around confused like. Sometimes I let one latch on, and then I pull it off and take it up on the bridge and play with it. "Just tormenting it," my mother would say. It's a stone bridge and the stones get pretty hot, too hot for me to sit on, so I 'm sure it's pretty uncomfortable for the bloodsuckers. They wriggle around, and I make sure they don't fall off back into the water. In the end I crush 'em with a rock, which is no easy thing because they are tough buggers.

Gray Towel

"Orville, come here!"

What did I do now? "Where are you?"

"In the bathroom; come here. You see this?"

"Yeah."

"What is this?"

"Soap."

"Do you know what it's for?"

"Yeah."

"Did you use it when you washed your hands?"

"Yeah, some."

"The soap is dry. Look at your towel. Look at it! It's gray. Here, wash your face with the wash cloth…and behind your ears and the back of your neck. Your neck is black. What on earth have you been into?"

"I don't know."

"What have you been doing this afternoon?"

"Playing in the hay."

"Well, you are disgustingly dirty. I'm going to get you black towels so they won't look so disgusting."

Games

"What on earth happened to your jeans? How did they get torn like that?"

"Cubby."

"Cubby tore your jeans?"

"Yeah. I throw a stick for him and when he runs after the stick I take off the other way and then he tries to catch me before I can climb a tree or the side of the barn. Sometimes he wins. It's a race."

"Why don't you throw the stick and race him to the stick?"

"He's faster than I am. I need a head start."

"You need a new pair of Levi's is what you need."

The race is the most excitin' game we play together. 'Nother thing we do is roll around on the ground wrestling and growling at each other. Prob'ly a good thing not too many people drive by 'cause when Cubby is on top they might think I'm being killed. When I make roads and such for cars and trucks, or a trench down the bank smooth enough to roll marbles, or a water siphon with dandelion stems, Cubby will be nearby watching, and when I change games or go to climb a tree for apples or pears or cherries or whatever is ripe, he sits right under the tree watching me. Once, when I got too far out on a apple tree limb and it broke, Cubby had to scramble to get out of the way. Come to think on it, I come down from a lot of trees that way—never get hurt though. Actually it's kinda fun.

It isn't all one way. Cubby has a game he plays alone while I watch. He chases cars. Whatever we're doin', when we hear a car Cubby takes up his favorite waiting-for-a-car position, hunkered down hidden from view, watching, waiting for the quarry. At just the right moment when the car is between banks on both sides of the road Cubby charges, hurling himself at the front tire snarling and barking, teeth bared. Even neighbors who are used to the attack sometimes get scared by how mean he seems barking with his teeth showing an' all, or they're afraid they might run over him. Cubby runs alongside pretending to bite the front tire and making quite a racket until the car has passed the house. I guess everybody thinks our house is well protected, but they might think different if they could see Cubby trotting back to me grinning from ear to ear, tongue lolling out the side of his mouth.

I Go On a Errand

"Orvie, would you please take the milk pail over to Gabavich's and get us some milk?"

"Aw, do I hafta? Tom Mix is coming on."

"No, you don't 'hafta' unless you want some ice cream."

"I scream, you scream, we all scream for ice cream."

"Here's the pail and money for the milk."

"It takes three quarters for a gallon of milk?"

"Yes. It costs a dime more at the store."

"Wow. I could get eight triple-scoop ice cream cones at Baker's for that. How many scoops will we get?"

"About that many from the cream and we'll have enough milk for a week. Now get along or you'll be late for Tom Mix."

The road is real dusty. Dad says he'll have to put water to the garden this weekend unless it rains. Think I'll lie on the stone bridge for a minute to see if I can see any fish. The stream doesn't have much water in it. The stones on the bridge are hot on my stomach. Feels kinda good. I'm getting that feeling again. There's still water running in the stream, but it sure is a lot less than in the spring. What splashed? There it is. Just a minnow.

The dust is so deep when I jump in it's kinda like jumping in a puddle of water the way the dust splashes away from my feet. Oh, wow! I never noticed that green stuff beside the road before. It's like real short grass, feels soft and smooth like that velvet cape in the attic I like to rub against. How come I never noticed it before. I'm gonna ask Mom what that green stuff is.

No cows in the pasture. They're all in the barn getting milked.

The Gabavich boys aren't really boys, they are men lots older than me, but they still live in the house where they grew up. They never went away for anything, school or the Army or got married or anything.

"Hi Orvie. You lookin' to get some milk?"

"Yeah. Here's the money."

"OK. Hang on a minute while I finish milking Nancy here."

The thing I like best about being around at milking time is all the cats sitting kinda lined up staring at Henry doing the milking. Every once in a while he aims a teat at one of 'em and shoots a stream of milk right at it. The cat sees it coming and opens her mouth and—squirt—she gets a mouthful. There are lots of cats around, which is better'n lots of mice and rats. We have cats too. Just about the first day after we moved to the farm a cat came around to the kitchen door and meowed and meowed and we felt sorry for her and put out a dish of milk. Mom said, "Poor thing; she looks like she's starving." Well, she was back the next night and got milk again, and the next night there were two cats and Mom put out more milk. Dad said if she kept putting out more milk every time another stray came around we'd be overrun with cats, so she just put out one dish every night. Other cats did come around, but it finally settled into just the first two: Whitey, who is all white, and Sniffer, who is black and white. Mom said she didn't know if we adopted them or they adopted us, but they were for sure our cats after that. They aren't allowed in the house, but they hang out here all the time. They look so happy with their feet curled under them lined up on the porch railing in the sun, and if I go near 'em they start to purr.

Henry takes the bucket full of milk and my pail into the milk room. After he takes the top off my pail he puts some cloth over it an' puts elastic around to hold the cloth in place, then he pours milk right out of his bucket into our milk pail.

"Why do you pour it through the cloth?"

"That's to filter out anything that might have got into the milk by mistake, like hair or a fly or anything."

"It doesn't look like there was anything."

"There usually isn't, but we can't be too careful."

"Do you filter all the milk?"

"Yep."

"Even those great big cans?"

"Yep. Thanks, Orvie. You be good now."

I don't know why people are always telling me to be good. I don't hardly even have a chance to be bad.

Wonder what I'd have to do to be bad?

Sex in Second Grade

We eat lunch at our desk, an' then we go outside if it's nice. On a nice day we really eat fast and run out unless the teacher is watching and makes us walk, but as soon as she can't see us we take off, out the door, across the porch, and down a bunch of stairs. At the bottom of the stairs, which I can jump in one leap, is a cement place that is flat. The girls play hopscotch there. We run around a lot at first an' go to the outhouse. There are two outhouses in back. The girl's is around the school one way and the boy's is around the other way, and straight behind the school is the ball field where the older kids in the other class-room usually play ball. We usually play Cowboys and Indians or Cops and Robbers. They're pretty much the same. We choose up sides and the Indians or the Robbers take off and hide out behind trees or the outhouses or rocks, and when the Cowboys or Cops come after them the Indians or Robbers shoot them and they shoot back until everybody is dead.

I don't always play those games. They're OK, but I get bored. Besides, mostly I like to be around girls. I don't know why, but I really like to look at girls, especially when they are jumping rope because their skirts and dresses fly up sometimes. I'm real interested in what's up there. Maybe I'm weird, I don't know, but I do know I'm not the only one. Jeffrey has a small mirror that he's always trying to get in a place where he can look up skirts. Sometimes he just puts it on the floor, and once he taped it to his shoe. The teacher told him more than once to put the mirror away, and once she kept him in at recess because he had it out again. I don't think she knows what he's doing with it. At least she hadn't said anything except, "Jeffrey, put that away," until finally one day she told him not to bring it to school again.

The girls let me jump rope with them. Mostly they like me to swing the rope, especially Sue May because she is taller than me even, and the swingers don't always get the rope high enough. It hits her head and then she's out, which isn't really fair because it isn't her fault. Sue May gave me half a Twinkie, and the other girls teased her and said she had a boyfriend, but I'm not anybody's boyfriend. I like to look at girls, but gosh they are weird sometimes. I mean, I really can't figure 'em out. They always have secrets and they aren't really nice to each other and they aren't nice to boys either, but they get really mad if boys aren't nice to them.

And what if Sue May was my girlfriend? What would that mean? Anyway, she isn't.

Rollie, Eric, and me were playing catch at recess yesterday when Big Jim called us over to the barrel where he was burning trash. There are two Jims in my school. The other Jim isn't Little Jim. He is just regular Jim. He's in fourth or fifth grade, I'm not sure, but he's in the other room with Mrs. Thornton. Big Jim is big, but he is only in first grade because he keeps being kept back. He'll be in first grade, I guess, until he gets to be sixteen, and then he won't have to go to school no more. He wipes the blackboards clean and claps the erasers and sweeps the cloakroom and stuff like that.

He is a moron, which means he won't ever get any smarter. He's a nice enough guy, but I can read better than he can and I'm about the worst reader in second grade. When we sit in a circle with our reading books and take turns reading, Big Jim only struggles through a couple of words before the teacher says, "Thank you, Jim," and goes on to the next person. I get through a couple of sentences, but it is really hard for me. Janet is Mrs. Holsapple's (we call her "Horse Apple" behind her back) pet, and she reads whole pages while the rest of us sit there and follow along, which is all right with me. But Mom doesn't think it's right, an' she ought to know, because she was a teacher before her an' Dad got married, in a one-room school where she had to teach all eight grades.

Anyway, Rollie, Eric, and me go over to see what Big Jim wants, and he shows us a little comic book he has that says it's the story of "Jack and Jill." It starts off with Jack and Jill going up the hill, and Jill has on a dress that's real short, and then they tumble down the hill and Jill's dress flies up and Jack can see her panties. I start to get a tingly feeling, and on the next page Jack is pulling down Jill's panties and they are kissing. Then Jill pulls off Jack's pants and he has a really big thing, if you know what I mean, and then they fuck—at least that's what I think they are doing. Nobody seems to know what that is exactly except that we aren't supposed to use the word, but I think that's what it is—Jack putting his thing between Jill's legs.

There aren't a lot of words, and I can read them all, and I think Big Jim can too. It's mostly "oww" and "ouch" when they roll down the hill and "let me see" and "kiss, kiss" and "oh" and "wow" and "you are so big" and then just like grunting sounds. They roll around on the ground and then at the end they get their clothes straightened out and they walk away together holding the bucket between them. Thing is, all the water must have spilled out of the bucket so I think they should've gone back up the hill.

We go back to playing catch, but it takes a while for the tingly feeling to go away. All three of us are pretty quiet. I guess Rollie and Eric are thinking about it same as I was.

I Get a Good Laugh

Dad an' me are sitting on the hood of the Jeep at the end of the road waiting for the bus. Grandma and Grandpa are coming for Thanksgiving. We hop off the hood when we see the bus and the bus driver stops with the door right in front of us. Grandma and Grandpa are both wearing hats, and Grandpa's wearing a suit and tie, and Grandma looks spiffy, too. Grandpa is carrying a suitcase and Grandma has a paper bag with handles. We all hug and Dad takes the suitcase and bag and puts them in the Jeep. Grandma and me climb into the back. I'm pretty sure the bag Grandma brought has something in it for me. I hope it's a toy or somethin' I can use 'cause I don't need no more clothes.

The Jeep only has two seats, and when we go anywhere I have to sit in the back on a kinda bench, which is over the wheels. I guess Dad knew that Grandma and Grandpa would be dressed up and that Grandma wouldn't want ta sit on Grandpa's lap and he wouldn't want her sitting on his lap anyway, so he took the cushions off the sofa and put 'em in the back to make a chair for Grandma, and she and I sit back there. She gives me a Archie comic from the bag. I like Archie comics because I think Veronica and Betty are ... well, sometimes they give me the tingly feeling that I don't tell anybody about. I like Veronica best.

Grandma and Grandpa are going to sleep in Mom and Dad's room, which has two beds right side by side, and Mom and Dad will sleep in the spare room, which has just one big bed. I stick right close to Grandma in case she has anything else in the bag. Mom gets 'em towels an' tells me to leave 'em alone while they "freshen up," whatever that means. I guess what it means is changing clothes, because when they come downstairs they are in more normal clothes. Grandpa goes out to look at the garden. Grandpa likes the farm. He don't really know anything about farming, but he likes to look at the chickens and the garden.

Grandma says she is a city girl, an' I guess she is, 'cause she always wears shoes with high heels on 'em. She never lived outside the city and she says she won't, ever. We have a good laugh on her when she asks Mom if there's anything she can do and Mom says to go out to the garden and get some beets. Well, she's used to buying 'em in bunches in the store, you know, and in the store they don't take the leaves off and they twist a green wire around the stems. She thinks that's the way they grow, in bunches, and she asks Mom how many bunches she should get. Ends up I go with her and she stands on the edge of the garden while I pull the beets.

We have chicken instead of turkey 'cause we have lots of chickens and don't have turkeys. Dad and me picked out a nice big rooster last night after they was all on the roost. Dad chopped his head off and put him in a bucket.

"Here, Orvie, take hold of his legs and hold on tight." The rooster was trying to kick, and his wings were thrashing around in the bucket something fierce.

"How come he doesn't just die?"

"He's dead enough, but his body doesn't know it yet. If we let it loose, it would run around, but I don't want it getting bruised or splashing blood all over the place."

"It stopped."

"Let's get that in boiling water so the feathers come out easier."

After we pluck the feathers off Dad cuts around what he calls the vent. It's where eggs and poop come out and if ya don't cut around it, it don't come out 'cause it's attached to the skin; course eggs don't come out of roosters. Next Dad cut a opening under what Mom calls the pope's nose and reaches in and pulls out the guts. He has to be careful not to mess up the liver 'cause it has a little green thing that, if you break it, it spoils the liver.

Mom chops up the heart and gizzard and sometimes the liver and calls them giblets and makes gravy with them. I like it best when she doesn't chop up the liver and instead fries it in butter. It's just a bite for everybody, but Grandma probably wouldn't like it so I could get hers.

The chicken smells so good when it's in the oven. It's my favorite way to have chicken. Everything else on the table is from the garden: potatoes, cabbage, carrots, Brussels sprouts (I don't like them so much but I always have to eat at least one), and beets. Oh, an' dessert is pumpkin pie and apple pie so people have a choice, which is great 'cause there is lots left over.

Grandma does have some more things in her bag for me: a bouncy ball that I can play catch with by bouncing it off the side of the barn and a Superman comic.

I Make a Snow Fort

"Dad, 'member the time we went sledding back where we lived?"

"I remember."

"And you told me to belly flop on top of you when you went past and you ran and belly flopped and I belly flopped on top of you?"

"And you got your hand under the runner, and I was worried you'd broken bones the way you were crying."

"But I didn't. I was crying because my decoder ring was crushed."

"I don't know if we'll be able to go sledding in this snow. It's pretty deep and still coming down, but maybe we'll be able to break a trail on the hill."

"I hope so."

It snows for almost two days, and the wind blows the snow around so's you can't hardly see the barn. When it stops snowing the road is pretty much filled up with snow. If somebody didn't know it was there, they might go walkin' along and slip down the bank and almost get covered up by snow. Dad an' me go out to the wagon shed to dig out the Jeep. Not that we can go anywhere 'cause the snow in the road is too deep an' Dad can't go to work.

"Dad! The snow is so high I can't hardly see over it."

"*Can* hardly see over it or can't see over it.

"I can almost see over it."

Dad laughed. "OK, Orvie, have it your way."

"Look! There ain't no snow next to the building."

"Hey, are you pulling my leg?"

"What?"

"What would your mother say?"

"That I shouldn't say 'ain't' and that 'ain't no' is a double negative, but I don't understand why 'hardly' is a negative."

"You'll have to ask your mother that one."

I help Dad shovel for a while, but then I get the idea to make a tunnel, not where the Jeep would go but under a drift that's even higher. I dig a neat fort with a big room I can sit in.

Mrs. Thornton to the Rescue

Oh, gosh! I've got my hand up as high as I can. I have to go so bad. Oh, oh, oh! Please, Oh, God, please, Mrs. Holsapple, please. Ow, ow, ow.

"Orville, sit down!"

I'm not really standing. I just want her to see that I have my hand up. Maybe she didn't see, but I have to go or I'll pee myself.

"What is it, Orville?"

"I have to go to the outhouse."

"Why didn't you go during recess?"

"I did, I think. I don't know."

"Ask properly."

"Can I please go to the outhouse?"

"May I."

"May I?"

"All right. Go ahead. Stand up straight and walk properly."

Oh, God, oh, God, oh, God....

"And don't run."

As soon as I get down the steps I run as fast as I can because the outhouse is all the way around in back, and I'm crying too because I'm afraid I'm not going to make it. Then I trip over a root and fall and scrape my hands and my knee hurts and I pee my pants and … oh, God. Everybody will know that I peed myself. I can't go back to class. I don't want to get on the bus where everyone will know what happened.

Mrs. Thornton is kneeling down beside me. She is the teacher in the other room. She teaches third, fourth, and fifth grade, and she'll be my teacher next year, and now she knows I peed myself.

"Orvie, what happened?" She is holding my hands and brushing the dirt and little stones off, which are all scratched and hurt.

"I had to go to the outhouse because I guess I forgot to go during recess and Mrs. Holsapple wouldn't let me go and I was running to try to get there in time and I tripped and fell."

"Well, let's get you inside and cleaned up." She takes me into her cloakroom and gets a washcloth and towel and a blanket and tells me to take off my wet pants and underpants and wipe myself off with the washcloth and dry myself and cover up with the blanket. Then she comes back and washes my hands, and I tell her my knee is bleeding, so she cleans and bandages that too. It turns out my knee got cut with a piece of coal. She puts iodine on my hands and knee, and it hurts a lot, but she blows on it and it feels better.

"Orvie, I put your clothes on the radiator to dry. Here are some books to read while you wait. I have to get back to my class now."

"What will Mrs. Holsapple do to me?"

"Now, don't you worry. I talked to her. She knows you are here. Everything will be fine."

I am worrying, not so much about Mrs. Holsapple but about the kids who will make fun of me. This is the worst day of my life, and I'll probably never have friends again or be allowed to play, and the girls will laugh at me. I'm crying again. I can't help it. Sitting in the cloakroom is something teachers sometimes make us do when we are bad, and I guess I deserve it. Just sitting there with the blanket wrapped around me looking at the books is awful boring, and I'm afraid school will let out and the bigger kids will come into the cloakroom to get their coats and I'll just be here with the blanket around me and no pants, but then Mrs. Thornton comes back with my pants and underpants.

"They're not quite dry, but they should be OK until you get home. Put them on and go back to your room."

When I go back to my room I'm surprised. The other kids aren't looking at me like they're going to make fun of me. They all look kinda serious, and Mrs. Holsapple looks serious and not as mean as she usually is. When the buses come and we're dismissed Rollie comes over and asks how I am, and I tell him about falling down and the cut on my knee where there was a hole in my pants and blood around it. I limp out to the bus. I guess everything's going to be OK after all, but I sure wish second grade could be over so I can be in Mrs. Thornton's room.

Stuck in the Mud

"Dad, 'member how you got stuck in the mud and the Jeep broke? How come there wasn't any mud on the road when I walked home from the bus?"

"Were there any jiggly places in the road when you were walking home?"

"Yeah, they're really neat. I like to jump in one place and see the road kinda roll; it's like throwing a stone in the water."

"Well, that's the mud, son. During the winter the ground freezes pretty deep, several feet. When it starts to thaw out the top dries and cars driving on the road pack it down and make it pretty solid, but below that when the frost in the soil thaws it turns into mud. When you jump on the road and it jiggles that's the mud jiggling."

"But it don't do that all the time."

"No, it *doesn't*, it only does it until all the ground thaws out. When the frost is completely out of the ground the water can drain out just like pulling the plug in the bathtub."

"How come you got stuck?"

"Well, I got out of the track that'd been packed down, and it wasn't as firm. Then one of the wheels broke through and I was in the soup. I put it in four-wheel drive, but the more I tried to get out the deeper I got."

"I thought the Jeep could get out of anything."

"So did I."

"Boy, you were really mad, Dad."

"Yeah, that was pretty stupid."

I Make a Mess

I like to sleep late; well, not sleep exactly but just stay in bed an' think about girls. I had a dream this morning about a girl in a pretty dress. She was just lying on her back on a real long, grassy bank. That's the dream. Nothin' else. She was pretty, and she was just lying there on the grass in the sun. I don't know why, but I had a stiffy and I just lay there on my stomach thinking about that girl an' how pretty she was an' kinda rubbing myself on the sheet, an' then there was a mess on the sheet an' I knowed that that was what was supposed to come out and not pee when I played with myself. I been thinking a lot about Jack and Jill.

The Ice is Gone

If I just push my foot into the mud ... squish, OK, good. Now I have a hollow I can fill with water if I make a canal to it from the stream. Hah! Now it's a swimming pool. Now all I gotta do is get something to put in my swimming pool. Tadpoles and minnows are good. Don't see any. Maybe under the bridge where it's shady. Water's still pretty cold.

I know, I'll catch some water bugs. I don't know how they do that, walk on water. It's not exactly walking; it's more like a canter. They look a lot like daddy-long-legs. Interesting. Their feet make dents in the water. It's like they are walking on a balloon instead of water.

Missed. They're fast. It's not really like a canter. It's more like skating. I'm going to call them water skaters. Dang it! They're fast. I know, I'll drop my shirt over it and then I can capture it for my swimming pool.

There, got it. It's in here someplace. Oh, damn.

OK, good. You won't get away this time. Ha! OK, here. You're going to like my swimming pool. Shoot! It goes on land as good as on water.

"Orvie! For goodness sake put on your shirt; you'll catch your death! What on Earth ... ? Come in the house and get on dry clothes."

Pancakes for Breakfast

"Get up, Orvie. Come on down here!"

I don't want to get up yet, but what is Dad up to? He should have gone for the train by now. The radio is on, which it never is in the morning. There's something goin' on. I haul myself out of bed, pull on my pants, and run downstairs. He's right at the bottom and he picks me up and throws me in the air. He's laughing and Mom is laughing and there is cheering on the radio. Dad holds me in one arm and puts his other arm around Mom and we start dancing around the kitchen an' Dad is singing, first time I ever heard him sing. "The war is over, the war is over, it's over over there, the war is over, the war is over, it's over over there." An' Mom starts singing too. On the radio I hear people shouting and cheering and the announcer talking about how everybody was about half crazy with joy.

We would have danced all day except we got tired and all three of us fell in a heap on the floor. Turns out because the Germans gave up Dad didn't have to go to work, so he made pancakes.

Soap

"Whatcha doin', Grandma?"

"Rendering fatback."

"From the pig?"

"Yep."

I ask her what rendering is, and she tells me it is cooking the fatback so it melts, which is lard, and she can skim off what doesn't melt.

"It stinks!"

"That's why I'm doing it outside." On our outside table she has a big pot on what we call a hotplate, which is like a electric stove with only one burner, and she has it plugged into a cord from the house.

"Are we going to eat it? 'Cause I don't think I wanna."

"You like pie, don't you?"

"Cherry pie's my favorite, but I don't think I'd like fatback pie."

She tells me lard makes good pie crust, and I can tell you she and mom make really good pies, but then she says she's going to make soap. That just doesn't make sense to me, that you can make soap out of greasy stuff that you would need soap to get off your hands. She allows as how I'm right about that, but she's going to mix the lard with lye. So I ask why we don't just wash with lye, and she says lye would eat the skin right off our bones.

"You need to be very careful with lye and make sure you don't get it on your skin. Now you skedaddle."

"I wanna watch you make soap."

"Go on boy, leave me be."

When she calls me "boy" I know I better mind, so I go around to the other side of the house and play with my soldiers for a while, but I really want to see her make soap so I go back and peek around the corner of the house. The fatback is still cookin' and she has a big flower pot set on a couple of boards that were set on the crock Dad makes sauerkraut in, and she has a bucket of water that I think she got from the rain barrel and is pouring it in the flower pot. She pours in some water, then goes to stir the fatback, then pours more water in the flower pot. I really want to ask her what she's doing but I know that's a bad idea, so I go back to my soldiers who were winning the war and killing all the Germans.

When I peek around the corner again she is just stirring the big pot.

"Orvie, get on over here."

"How did you know I was there?"

"I have eyes in the back of my head. Here, stand on this chair and stir the pot. Stir it nice and slow and don't get it up on the sides of the pot. That's a boy, just like that."

"Where's the lye, Grandma?"

"It's in there. All we have to do now is stir it until it makes soap."

"Where'd the lye come from?"

"See these ashes in the flower pot? When I poured water

over ashes it took the lye out of the ashes. Now, you keep stirring while I clean up around here."

"Grandma, I'm getting tired."

She takes the spoon and stirs really fast and then scrapes the soap off the sides of the pot and hands the spoon back to me. "Keep stirring, nice and slow."

"How much longer?"

"Never mind, boy, just keep stirring."

After she cleaned up there's nothing left on the table 'cept the pot sitting on the hotplate. Then she comes back with a pan of water and takes the spoon from me .

"Watch this Orvie. She holds the spoon over the water and lets some of the soap drip onto the surface. Wow! The drops of soap zip around on the water faster than anything, like water bugs, only white. It would be swell if I could use the soap drops to make a speedboat go so I find a little piece of shingle and I make one end pointy and put a notch in the other end put it in the water and ask Grandma to drop some soap in the notch. She does but it doesn't really work all that great. The boat just spins around a little and the soap takes off in another direction.

Grandma says that's enough and I should stir some more. She dumps the water out and spreads a dish towel over the pan and pushes the edges down all around, then she takes up the stirring.

"How did you learn to make soap?"

"My momma taught me."

Pretty soon she says the soap is ready and she pours it into the pan right on top of the dish towel and says that's all there is to it.

"That doesn't look like soap."

"Sure it does."

"It looks more like jello with milk in it."

"When it dries out in a day or two I'll cut it into bars and then it will dry out some more and you will have lots of soap to keep clean behind your ears."

If we're going to start talkin' about washing behind my ears, it's time for me to skedaddle. I bet soldiers don't have to wash behind their ears.

Thunder Bridge

My favorite color is chickweed. In my whole box of crayons there's no chickweed color. Violet is the closest, but chickweed is bluer than violet but it's not blue. I never seen chickweed color in the sky. But ya can't see the color now with all the dust on the flowers. Not all that many cars go by but they sure make a lot of dust, an' everything along the road is covered with it, 'cept the poison ivy. Dust don't stick to poison ivy.

I'm real lucky. I don't get poison ivy 'cept if I get into it and I have a scratch. Then the scratch gets the itchy bumps but that's the only place. I'm sure glad I'm not like Gwendolyn. They say if she even looks at poison ivy she'll get all-over bumps. Before school starts her dad comes by and scouts out all around the school to make sure there ain't no poison ivy. She couldn't even be walking down the road like I am.

Ah, there's a real good stick for a fishing pole. Gosh, the dust is thick. I don't think I ever seen it so thick. That time the plane crashed in the field here it was pretty thick and that was pretty crazy. I heard the plane real low and I thought it might be our friend Don Hick, 'cause he has a plane and he landed in our field once. Before he landed he flew low over the house two or three times and we went out and waved at him and he wiggled the wings to wave back. We didn't think he would land but he did. That was pretty exciting.

Mom thought he was crazy because his wheel might have hit a woodchuck hole and that would have wrecked him, but he said he could see OK enough to miss the holes because we had mowed the field.

Anyway, the plane that wrecked right here in Johnson's field wasn't trying to land. He was trying to fly under the telephone wire and he didn't make it. He was kinda braggin' that he almost made it but the tail part just barely snagged the wire. I got a souvenir back in my room. It's a piece of the propeller. It's almost a foot long and real shiny wood. When I heard the plane and went out to see it it was so low I didn't see it and then I heard the crash and went running down the road. The pilot wasn't hurt but his plane sure was. We all thought he was pretty stupid for trying a trick like that.

Johnson's house is always quiet. Mr. Johnson gets some farming done, but I almost never see him around. He lives in the house with his mother but I never seen her neither.

This here bridge across the brook is the best place for gigging suckers. Suckers don't ever bite at a worm or grasshopper or anything. I've dropped hooks with all kinds of bait on them, even baloney and pieces of bread right in front of 'em, and they just sit there not movin', but as soon as I drop a triple hook, they move away. Well, not always because I do pretty good gigging them but I best get them with the first try or it gets a lot harder.

There's a cement platform under the bridge that's wide enough for me to sit on. It's nice here under the bridge, kinda like a cave, and it's the best place to get suckers 'cause my shadow don't scare 'em 'cause I'm under the bridge. When a car comes they drive right over my head and they don't know I'm there unless I stick my head out to see who it is, but I can usually know who it is by the sound their car makes. The tires on the bridge sound like thunder, or a crashing airplane. Ha. Ha.

Oh, good, three suckers hanging out. I don't need the pole. Just drop the hook in real slow…come on, sink, you bastard. Damn, the string is floating. Gotta get it wet. Be better if I had a weight.

A Grownup Celebration

Dad comes home with a bottle and some cheese an' is all excited because the war is over.

"I thought the war was over before."

"That was the war in Europe," Dad says. "The war in the Pacific was still going on until now."

"What's the Pacific?"

"That's the ocean on the other side of our country. We have the Atlantic between us and Europe, and the Pacific is between us and Japan. The Japs have given up and the war is over. This was the war to end all wars. You won't ever have to worry about war in your life."

Well that sounds real good to me 'cause war sounds like a really bad thing. The bottle is somethin' called Creme de Cacao. Dad and Mom start dancin' around in the kitchen and Dad's holding the bottle all the time and then they hug me. He pours cream off the top of the milk into two funny little glasses and then he pours the Creme de Cacao real careful down the side of the glass so it goes to the bottom without getting mixed in. He says that's the way to do it 'cause the brown stuff is heavier than the cream and sinks to the bottom but if he tried to float the cream on top of the brown stuff it would get mixed up.

Then Mom and Dad clink glasses and say, "Here's to Harry," and take a sip.

"Who's Harry?" I ask.

Mom says, "He's the president, and he dropped the biggest bomb ever made on Japan. And when they didn't give up he dropped another one." I thought Mom didn't like the president but I guess even bad presidents can do good things sometimes.

"Can I have some?"

"*May* I have some, and no, you may not. It's not for little boys."

"It's a celebration," Dad says, "the end of the biggest war the world has ever seen. I guess a sip won't do any harm. Here, just a sip. It's very strong and you might not like it."

"I like it! It tastes like chocolate milk only better! May I have some more?"

"No, son, it's a grownup drink. We wouldn't want you to get sick."

That tastes so good, I can't wait to get grown up.

Bad Words

"Dad, what's a bad word?"

"Bad word? Why are you asking?"

"Well, we were talking on the bus and everybody was sayin' what they weren't allowed to say at home because they were bad words."

"What were some of the words?"

"You know. The words you tell me not to say when Grandma is around—God damn and shit and like that. An' Eddie said 'ain't' because it's not in the dictionary and Howard said it was, and then I said 'don't,' which kinda stumped everybody. Why are you laughing?"

"Sorry, buddy, I couldn't help myself. Howard was right. 'Ain't' is in the dictionary, but it's just not good English, which is why educated people don't use it. 'Don't' is a perfectly fine word."

"Every time I say it Mom makes me say 'doesn't.'"

"Not every time. It's the way you use it. 'It don't matter,' is incorrect, But, 'I don't have time,' is correct."

"Why?"

"I don't know. Ask your mother."

"Howard said his mother told him he shouldn't say 'moron.' Why is that a bad word?"

"You know what the word means?"

"Yeah. Big Jim is a moron. It means not very smart."

"Do you call Big Jim a moron?"

"No."

"Why not?"

"I don't know, guess it'd hurt his feelings."

"Do you call anybody else a moron?"

"Yeah."

"Why?"

"Because they're being a jerk and acting stupid."

"You know they aren't really morons?"

"Yeah."

"You ever call someone a moron where Big Jim might hear?"

"I don't know. Maybe."

"How would that make Big Jim feel?"

"I don't know. Bad, I guess."

"Do you want to make Big Jim feel bad?"

"No."

Dad goes back to shoveling manure out of the barn and I pick a scab off my knee that itches.

"How come you don't tell me there are bad words?"

"I don't think there are bad words; there are bad thoughts and people do bad things, but the words aren't bad."

"You mean like what we say when someone calls us a name: 'sticks and stones can break my bones but words can never hurt me?'"

"Well, not exactly. Words can be hurtful. That saying works for you if someone calls you a moron because you aren't, but it might hurt Jim."

"Why don't you just tell me that 'moron' is a bad word and I shouldn't use it?"

"Would that work?"

"I don't know. Maybe."

"Does it work with your friends?" He had me there. "If I just said something was a bad word and not to use it, you might use it anyway because you didn't know why I thought it was a bad word. Seems to me it's better to talk about things."

"So, it ought to be up to me when I use 'don't.'"

I run away 'cause I think he's going to pitch a shovel full of manure at me.

Treasure Island

I'm really glad I'm in Mrs. Thornton's class. Not that she's easy or anything. Mostly, I guess, I'm just glad I'm not in Mrs. Holsapple's class anymore, and that was a close call, I'll tell you. She was going to keep me back because I couldn't read good enough. I was afraid I would end up like Big Jim, who was just about old enough so he didn't have to go to school anymore. I sure didn't want to be in her class clapping erasers and sweeping up for the rest of my life, but Mom and Dad talked to Mrs. Holsapple and they got her to pass me.

Mrs. Thornton has third, fourth, and fifth grades. There are six rows of desks, two rows for each grade, and I'm in the last desk of the second row, which I like because there's nobody behind me and I can see everybody. If somebody wants to throw a spitball at me they have to turn around in their seats so their backs are turned to the teacher, but when I'm shooting spitballs I have the whole room in front of me so I can keep my eye on her. She still catches me sometimes, even when I could swear she's not looking. I know it's not possible but it seems like she's got eyes in the back of her head like my grandma said.

One day I just didn't wanna be in class at all. Mrs. Thornton was teaching geography or something to fourth and fifth grade. I was s'posed to be answering questions about a story we had just read, but I didn't really understand the questions and the story was boring, about somebody raking leaves and kids hiding in the piles. I scrunched down in my seat and then slipped onto the floor and crawled to the closet in the back of the room. It was kind of exciting to be in the closet where I wasn't supposed to be and the teacher not missing me or knowing where I was, but then that got boring too.

There were all sorts of things in the closet: crayons, paper, a big box full of little boxes of chalk, and a box of brand-new board erasers, but mostly books. There was an old book there—really old. The cover was falling off and the pages all turning brown and kind of crumbling on the edges. It had pictures of pirates, a pirate with one leg holding a telescope and with a parrot on his shoulder, a boy wearing a triangle hat on a dock and lots of sailing ships. Under one picture I read, "No lives were lost, and we could wade ashore in safety," and under another one where a man with a knife was attacking the boy it said "...when I looked around, there was Hands, already halfway toward me...." The title was *Treasure Island* and I started reading it 'cause I wanted to know more about the boy, Jim Hawkins, and the one-legged man.

"Orvie, what are you doing in here?"

"Oh, gosh, Mrs. Thornton. I'm sorry."

"It's time to get on the bus. We'll talk about this Monday."

"Yes, ma'am. Can I read this book?"

"*Can* you? It's pretty advanced for you."

"I really like it."

"Well, I never. Yes, Orvie, you *may* read it."

"Can I take it home?"

"Yes, you *may* take it home. Now get going or you'll miss the bus."

I read the book all the way home. There were some words I didn't understand, but I just kept going and it just kept getting more interesting. After I got off the bus I tried to read it while walking, but it slowed me down so much and I was afraid it might fall apart if I didn't hold it careful, so I just hurried home.

"Orvie, what are you doing there?"

"Reading."

"Reading? Where did you get that book?"

"Mrs. Thornton gave it to me."

"And you're reading that big book?"

"Yeah."

"Don't you want something to eat?"

"I'm OK."

"Now, Bill, sit where you are," said the beggar. "If I can't see, I can hear a finger stirring. Business is business. Hold out your right hand. Boy, take his right hand by the wrist, and bring it near to my right."

We both obeyed him to the letter, and I saw him pass something from the hollow of the hand that held his stick, into the palm of the captain's, which closed upon it instantly.

"And now that's done," said the blind man; and at the words he suddenly left hold of me, and, with incredible accuracy and nimbleness, skipped out of the parlor and into the road....

Monday at school Mrs. Thornton didn't scold me at all and actually let me read *Treasure Island* most of the day except for when we said the Pledge of Allegiance and when we sang and when I had to do arithmetic. She didn't actually say I could read it, but I'm pretty sure she knew what I was doing. I finished the book before the end of the week, reading on the bus and whenever I could. It was a swell story and I think anyone who wants a good book ta read would like it.

Jim Hawkins is the hero of the book an' he's a boy maybe a little older'n me. It's kind of interesting that Long John Silver is a bad guy but he didn't kill Jim when he had the chance, and ya kinda don't mind that he gets away at the end.

> *"Fifteen men on the dead man's chest—*
> *Yo-ho-ho, and a bottle of rum!"*

Breakfast

"Mom, I want cereal for breakfast this morning."

"May I please?"

"May I please have cereal?"

We usually have eggs because not all of the eggs the chickens lay are fertile, and the hospital in New York that we sell eggs to hatches 'em for research. Every egg has to have the number of the chicken on it. Ya see, the way it works is all the chickens have metal bands on their legs with a number. The nests where they lay their eggs are called trap nests. When the chicken goes into the nest a door closes and locks her in until Mom or Dad or me let her out. When we open the nest we check the number on her leg and write it on the egg with a pencil, and we check her off on a big chart that she laid an egg that day. We do that so we can see if there's a chicken that's not laying at all, and then we find her and eat her since there's no sense feeding a chicken that isn't laying. Here's another help at finding them: usually chickens with small combs are the poor layers.

We put the eggs in a special padded metal case that holds ten dozen eggs, and either Dad takes it to New York with him or we give it to Mr. Crosby and he delivers it. At the hospital Dad says they inject (look it up if you don't know what that means) things into some of the eggs, and some of them they don't do anything to. They call those the control eggs so they can see if what they injected did anything—you know, made the chickens sick or strange or anything. That way they hope they will figure out what causes cancer.

If none of the eggs that they injected hatch, that's not our fault, but they keep records on each chicken just like we do, except they mark down which eggs hatch and which don't, and if one of the numbers don't hatch regularly they tell us they don't want eggs from that chicken anymore. That chicken is still laying eggs but her eggs aren't fertile. I don't know if she doesn't like roosters or if the roosters don't like her but, whatever, her eggs end up on our breakfast table or we sell 'em.

"Neato! Look, it's a circus wagon with a lion in it."

"Don't you already have one of those?"

"Nah-uh, the one I have has monkeys in it."

Shredded Wheat has cardboard things in between every three biscuits to keep them separate and there's always something interesting on the cards, like this one is a lion in a circus wagon I can cut out and fold to make it look like a real model wagon. Sometimes it's just interesting stuff to read, like the picture of a Coast Guard cutter an' all about it, but its best when there are things to cut out and paste and color. Shredded Wheat has a picture of Niagara Falls on the box, which Dad has seen. He said he drove there in a Model T Ford in 1928 an' it took two days from Philadelphia. He said he got a flat tire 'cause the roads were so bad. He said he'd take me there sometime. If you haven't seen it, it is a really big waterfall up near Canada.

"Mom, please pass the sugar." Mom puts honey on her biscuits but I like sugar, same with grapefruit. Mom says I used to like honey, but when I was three I climbed up onto the counter and got into the honey jar and ate the whole jar with my finger and upchucked and I don't like honey anymore. Mom says I have to go easy on the sugar 'cause it's rationed an' she can't always get it. That's 'cause of the war, but I figure I should be able to use more sugar now 'cause the war is over.

What I do with the shredded wheat biscuits (I usually have two) is I put sugar on 'em and then milk, and then I take an' cut them down the middle with my spoon. Then it's easy to just cut off spoon-size bites.

I would rather have cow's milk, except in the spring when the wild onions in the pasture look like grass to the cows, I guess, cause the milk tastes like garlic, but we have to use goat's milk most of the time except when Nanny is nursing kids.

Goats, by the way, well, I just don't like 'em all that much. First off, they will eat anything, but especially they like the garden and the fruit trees we planted last year, so they have to be kept chained up when they aren't in the barn; so every morning someone has to clip a chain on their collar and take them out to pasture where the chain's fastened to a pipe stuck in the ground. You can pretty much figure that once or twice a day you will hear one of them bleating as if they were being choked to death and, sure enough, they are. They'll have got the chain wound around something until it is just a knot of chain and their head is tied down right to the ground and they are on their knees. Wouldn't ya think that when their chain kept getting shorter they would figure out to turn around and go the other direction? I mean, for goodness sake!

Dam

"Orvie! What on earth have you been up to?"

"Whaddya mean?"

"You're all wet and muddy."

"Oh, I been making a dam."

"Where?"

"By the stone bridge."

I been working on damming up the stream to make a pond and it's been hard work, I'd say. First, I put in some stones and they held back some water but lots went through because of the spaces between them; so then I looked around for a big rock. I figured if it was just one rock blocking the stream, water couldn't run through that so I started looking around for one. I found some mostly in the ground, so I got a shovel from the tool shed and tried to pry some up, which wasn't easy, but I finally got a pretty good one out of the ground. Trouble was I couldn't lift it and it didn't roll too good either. I was wishin' I had a wagon or somethin. I thought of my sled, but I didn't think I could get it on the sled, and even if I did I was afraid it would fall off. Then I thought of the corrugated tin sheets that used to be on one side of the outback shed but fell off. Dad had replaced them with boards. Last winter I turned up one end of one of 'em and used it like a toboggan. I sprang into action and fetched it and was able to get the rock onto it, but it was hard to pull because the edges hurt my hands an' I couldn't pull so good bent over, so I got a piece of rope and the hammer and chisel and I banged two holes in the tin and made a tow rope just like I have on my sled. Then I put the rope around my shoulders, my back actually, well the back of my shoulders, and I pulled backing up, which turned out to be the best way to do it.

It took a while but I got the rock to the edge of the stream and I rolled it right in. I pushed it around and wiggled it and jumped on it to get it just right, and finally the water started backing up a little bit but then it could run around the rock. I started filling in on the sides of the rock with stones, but I knew that wouldn't work too good. That's when Mom called me for lunch.

"Get out of those wet clothes and wash up."

During lunch I tell her what I've been up to and ask her to come see what I've done. She doesn't want me to put my wet sneakers back on, but I don't have any other shoes and it's still too cold to go barefoot, so she allows as how I'll be all right with dry socks on. I can't wait to get back and see how big my pond is. It's a little bit bigger, I think, but the stones aren't really holding back much water.

"Why, Orvie, that's really quite a project you've got there. That is a true Boulder Dam."

"Yeah, but the water runs through the stones. I want a bigger dam but it's no good with the water running through like it is. I wish I had some cement."

"How would you get the cement to harden?"

"I don't know but I'd figure something out."

"How about you use dirt?"

"I tried that but it just turns to mud and then it washes right out."

"How about clumps of sod?" I'm not quite sure what she means, but she takes the shovel and digs up some grass with its roots. I scrape away the stones on one side of the boulder and press the sod into the space.

"Mom, you're a genius!"

"Try not to get too dirty." She is grinning when she heads back to the house, I guess because she thought she was so smart.

Now here is something I learnt that you will want to know if you ever build a dam. You can't stop a leak on the downstream side. That's where you see the water coming through, but no matter how much stuff you push into that hole and how hard you push it in the water is gonna get through. Ya gotta find the upstream side of the hole, but it's not just on the other side of where the water's comin' through. Here's a trick I learnt: I took a fistful of mud and moved it around in the water near where the leak was until muddy water came through the leak, and then I pushed the mud into that place until the leak stopped.

I was telling Dad about this, and he said I had learned something that would be valuable to me for my whole life. I told him I didn't think I'd be building dams my whole life, but he said the lesson was that when I have a problem I should try to look for the source of the problem rather than trying to patch it up on the face. Then he got into talking about government and politicians and I kinda got bored.

Tracking Indians

Ya gotta be real quiet when you're tracking Indians; careful like Deerslayer not to step on a stick and make it crack, because Indians can hear real good and they will come and get us. Cubby, my faithful scout, and me are heading up the mountain to the woods, but first we have to cross the raging river. I wish we had a canoe like Deerslayer. We go along the bank looking for a way to get across and we come to a tree with some big branches that reach across the river. Deerslayer stealthily climbs the tree and walks out on a branch holding onto a branch above. Faithful scout plunges into the rushing water, takes a drink of the clear, cold water, and swims across, climbing the bank just as Deerslayer drops out of the tree next to him.

"Hey! Jeez, Cubby, do ya have to shake the water off right next ta me? I'm soaked! I might as well've waded across."

The trail through the dense underbrush is hard to follow. There are deer tracks in the squishy soil but we don't see any moccasin prints. Indians are real smart. They can run for miles without stopping or making any noise or leaving a trail. Sometimes when they do leave footprints they take a branch and sweep the trail so the prints can't be seen and trackers can't follow 'em. I know their tricks though so I stay on the trail.

I wonder if this Indian has a squaw. I wonder what she

wears. I saw a picture on a calendar at the garage of a Indian kinda passed out on a sheet tied between two trees and a Indian woman in a short buckskin skirt and a real curvy body standing next to him, and it said, "A buck well spent on a Springmade sheet," which was pretty funny. I'd sure like to see a Indian like that.

> *Jack and Jill went up the hill*
> *To fetch a pail of water.*
> *Jack fell down and broke his crown.*
> *Jill came tumbling after.*

> *Jack saw panties and went crazy*
> *Chasing Jill around.*
> *Jack and Jill rolled on the ground*
> *And Jack loved what he found.*
> *I'm a poet*
> *An' don't know it.*

At the top of the mountain there is a dense forest of pine trees. I think I'd like to be an Indian now because the white man is clever, but I have a way to trick him so not even his tracker dog can follow me. I fight my way through a few of the trees with their branches so close they touch each other. I climb a tree to the very top where it is real sway-ey and start swinging it back and forth until I can reach the top of the next tree, which I grab and then leap across to. This way I can travel across the pine forest without leaving a trail of any kind. Not even a bloodhound could follow the scent.

Up there it's like being a bird 'cause all I can see are the tops of the pine trees. Nobody else has ever done this—leastways I never read about it or heard it or anything. The trees were planted by Mr. Morris all in rows and close together. I think he was going to sell Christmas trees, but then he died and the trees just kept getting taller. Sometimes I see a bird sitting on the very top of a tree, which is almost where I am.

I swing across the treetops, eluding the cowboys who are trying to capture me. It's time to get back down to good ol' solid ground, so I climb carefully down, dropping quietly to the ground where my faithful trained wolf, Scout, is sitting waiting for me. He has been able to track the crafty Indian using his keen senses of smell and hearing.

Coming out of the dense pine trees into a forest where the ground is covered with leaves makes me think of the girls at school playing in a pile of leaves Jim had raked up. They were jumping in the leaves and throwing leaves at each other and their skirts kind of flew up; I wish they had flown up higher 'cause I didn't really see anything.

The leaves were squashed down by snow over the winter and aren't crunchy, a lucky thing for Scout and me. But still, we need to be careful. When I walk I put down the side of my foot first and then roll onto the rest of my foot because even the thump of a foot can be heard far off. I stop and put my ear to the ground and sure enough I feel the vibration of someone walking, probably a Mohican. We better stop and pitch camp where we can't be seen. There is a big branch down, a perfect place to make a fort and plenty of smaller branches and sticks lying all around to pile and weave into a really good fort. When I'm finished Scout and I sit in it to wait until the coast is clear. I get that tingly feeling because it's so cozy and I think about the girls playing in the leaves again.

"Orvie, where have you been?" Mom is standing on the porch. Cubby runs ahead. "I've been calling and calling. I was getting worried."

"Cubby and me...."

"Cubby and I."

"Cubby and I was up...."

"Were."

"...were up the hill in the woods. We built a neat fort. I think I could make it so it would keep out rain and snow and be warm in the winter."

"You must be hungry. Come inside and have an apple." I was hungry, and when I went inside the smell in the kitchen made me even hungrier. There was a pot on the stove and the lid was making a popping noise.

"You know the pine woods Mr. Morris planted back before he died, you know, for Christmas trees?"

"Yes."

"I climbed up one of the trees almost to the top and I got it swinging back and forth and I reached out and grabbed the top of another tree and I just swung across into that tree and then I did it again and again."

"You went from one tree to another without climbing down?"

"Yeah. It was neat."

"Well, I declare, that is something. You be careful, though. Remember the branch that broke when you were too far out on the limb?"

"Yeah, that was just a apple tree and I wasn't very high and the branch didn't really fall but just kinda cracked and went down slow."

"*An* apple tree. Still, those pines are pretty tall. I don't want you getting hurt."

"Don't worry, Mom, I'm a superior tree climber."

Bugs Are a Lot of Fun

"I need some pins, Mom."

"What are you up to this time?"

"I'm going to make a jail for flies outta this cork."

"You may take some pins from the pin cushion next to my sewing machine, but don't take too many."

I'll hollow out the cork with my knife and then put the pins into the cork all around the edge close enough so a fly can't get between the bars. When I get a fly I'll pull up one of the pins, put the fly in, and close the jail again. Or maybe it's a cage like in a zoo or at the circus and the fly is a caged animal.

It takes a lotta skill to catch a fly. The first time I caught one in school I became kinda a hero. The other guys wanted to know how to do it, so I showed them but most of them gave up, all except Smitty and Roland. Once you get the hang of it you can get a fly on the first swipe most o' the time. Watcha do when a fly lands on your desk is ya cup your hand and sneak up 'til you're pretty close without ya spook the fly and then ya swoop across a couple of inches above the fly and close your fist when you feel your palm hit the fly. Once ya got it in your fist ya throw it down on the floor or your desk or the road or some other hard place to stun it. Then you can pick it up and do whatever ya want.

Oh, darn. I guess I'll only be able to have one fly in the cage cause the first one got out while I was puttin' the second one in.

Sometimes I take off one wing and watch 'em try to fly when they wake up. Other times I take off both wings and put them on a piece of wood or a leaf or something and put them in the brook or in a pan of water. I like to get two leaves or somethin' else flat and put flies without wings on them and set them off together and imagine they are sailing around the world in a race. I don't drop 'em from the bridge but put 'em in next to each other. I like to put three flies on one and one on the other and see if they ever get close enough that one of the flies crosses over to the other ship. It hasn't happened yet, but it might.

Cicadas are the most fun of all. I look for them every year. It's easy to know when to look because they make so much noise. They're a lot easier to catch than flies. Seeing them is the hard part, but once I find one I just cup my hand over it and pick it up. It tickles when it tries to fly. I hold it by the head and tie a string around its body under the wings then let it go. It flies around but can't get away because I'm holding the string. It's like having a toy airplane that really flies.

Cucumber beetles love to hang out in squash flowers, which is the best place to catch 'em. I mostly just pull off the whole flower and start squashing them in the flower. They aren't real easy to kill in there because they have hard shells and the flower is squishy, so I have to squeeze hard and kind of chop through with my thumbnail. Dad says the flowers with all the beetles in there look like a French whorehouse. I asked him what he meant and he said the bright orange and yellow were lurid and the center of the flower with the pollen on it looks like velvet. He told me I'd have to look up "lurid," but I still don't get it.

"Dad, did you know girl beetles are bigger than the boy beetles?"

"Really? How do you know that?"

I pick a blossom and show him. "See, there are three couples in there and the smaller one is always on top."

"Well I'll be darned. I suppose the ones that aren't mating are waiting their turn." We laugh at that and then I tell him I laugh sometimes when they know I'm after them and the girl beetle will start running or she will let go and drop. It seems like the boy beetles never see me coming. They never stop what they're doin'. It must be a shock to be havin' fun like that an' all of a sudden you're falling and then landing and then the girl you are on is runnin' around trying to hide but you just hang on and keep doing what you were doing.

We laugh some more and then I tell him about flies; when you catch 'em you can sex 'em, tell their sex I mean. It's fun to sex flies in school 'cause everybody's pretty interested. To sex a fly you put him on his back and push a pencil point into his gut. If it's a male, you will see something pop out of his backside, an' when you take the pencil away the thing goes back inside. If it don't go back inside, it's a female and you pushed too hard and her guts popped out. The girls go all "eww" and "gross" but everybody laughs.

Not All Bugs Are Fun

I can run on the road in my bare feet an' it doesn't hardly hurt, 'cause my feet are so tough they're like leather. It hurts a little walkin' in the field after it's been mowed because the stubble scratches the sides of my feet, but the worst of all happened to me yesterday when I was walkin' on the lawn to the wagon shed. The problem was there's a lot of clover in the lawn, and bees like clover, so—you guessed it—I stepped on a bee. I ran to the house hollering.

There is one class of insects that you kinda watch out for, the stinging kind. I knew better. I been stung before but I guess I was thinking of something else. You got bees—bumble and honey—wasps, and yellow jackets. The yellow jackets are the only ones that really bother me because they are sneaky. I don't guess they are really sneaky, but they sure surprise me more than the others. They live in the ground, an' ya can be walking along whistling an' just enjoying yourself even watching where ya were going an' all of a sudden *zzzzzz* an' a yellow jacket is stinging ya and others come an' they don't stop. The only thing ta do is run like hell. Ya also gotta watch out for 'em in the orchard when there are apples on the ground.

Bees are too busy to bother a body unless a body bothers them. Like when I 'm going after cucumber beetles that are in the squash blossoms, there are always (well almost always) bees in the blossoms too. I can stick my knife into the blossom to coax the beetles out, and the bees don't care. They don't pay me no-never-mind. Sometimes they bump against my hand when they fly out, which would prob'ly scare a lot of folks, but if you just go about your business and let them go about theirs there's no problem. But if you start jumping around and swatting at the bee to keep it away, oh, brother, you're askin' for it.

Dad says bees are important, especially in the orchard but in the garden too because they pollinate the flowers. I told you about the male and female cucumber beetles. Well, the squash plants have male and female flowers, too. They are even easier to tell. First, the male is just on a stem sticking up while the female is on the end of a little squash. Second, if you look into the flower the male looks like a boy, if you know what I mean. The female is more complicated to describe. Anyway, they are different, and anyone who has looked into a few squash flowers can tell the difference. I'm not sure how it all works, but I know it's important for bees to spread the pollen (it's like dust) from one flower to another. I just wish they didn't like clover flowers.

Mom put baking soda on my foot where the bee stung me and I'm OK today, but, boy, that hurt.

Wasps, I don't know what they do that's good. I've been stung by 'em, too, but usually it's because I didn't run fast enough when I was knocking down their nest.

A Surprise Visitor

Cubby is watching me burn ants with a magnifying glass when all of a sudden he jumps up and starts barking. I look where he is lookin' and there's a man in a suit and tie and hat comin' up the road, and then I realize who it is.

"Grandpa! Grandpa!" I run to meet him as he crosses the bridge. "Grandpa, how did you get here? Where's Grandma? Are you staying? What's in the bag?"

Grandpa doesn't talk much, but he lets me hold his hand while we walk up the hill. Mom comes out of the house to see what Cubby was barking about.

"Land sakes, Charles, this is a surprise! How did you get here?"

My Grandpa's name is same as my middle name, and my name is the same as my father's, which is mostly OK, 'cept when someone calls my father Orvie and then I think they mean me and it gets confusing. I hardly ever see my Grandpa except when we visit him and Grandma at their house in Philadelphia. He smokes a pipe, which I think smells real good, and reads the paper and listens to *One Man's Family* on the radio and winds the clock every night before going upstairs to bed. I like to hear his voice because it is real soft and low, kinda like bees in the orchard.

He says he took the bus, and it let him out at the end of the road where our road comes out on the concrete road, and he walked all the way.

"Why that's more than three miles, Charles. Why didn't you let us know you were coming? We could have picked you up."

He says he hadn't really planned to come, but it was just a nice day and he wanted to get out of the city. Then Mom asks if he is hungry and he says no and she says he must be starving and she makes up a plate of meatloaf left-over from last night and some other stuff and he eats it right up.

"Where's Margaret?" Mom asks. That's my Grandma.

"Home."

I think Mom wants to know why she didn't come, too, but decides not to ask any more. I want to know what's in the brown paper bag he's carrying.

"Socks and underwear."

If Grandma had come, there would have been something for me. She always has something swell for me when she comes or when we visit them. For my birthday she sends a big box, and inside the box are lots of little presents like a package of balloons, some soldiers, and cars and trucks. This year I got a tube of plastic stuff that I put a blob of on the end of a straw and could blow up a big bubble almost as big as a balloon. But the socks and underwear aren't even for me. They're clean clothes for Grandpa.

Pretty soon after Dad gets home we get a phone call from Grandma. She says she's worried sick because she doesn't know where Grandpa is, and when Dad tells her he's here with us she gets mad, and then Grandpa won't get on the phone to talk to her, which makes her madder still. Turns out they'd had a fight about some "silly little thing," at least that's what Mom and Dad said.

Grandpa stayed for three days. He washed his underwear and socks in the bathroom sink every morning and hung them on the line. He didn't wear his hat or tie until he left to go home, and he mostly sat on the porch smoking his pipe. I sat with him sometimes, mostly where I could smell the pipe smoke.

The Mail

"Come on, Cubby. Let's go wait for the mailman. Sit. Good dog."

We sit on the stone steps that go down the bank to the mailbox. I guess that when they made the road they dug it out some, because the road is lower than where our house is and on the other side where the garden is, too. It's a lot like the banks of the brook. It's nice just sitting here with Cubby waiting for Mr. Crosby.

"Look at the ants, Cubby." It looks like they're going back and forth on a little ant road. Ants run all the time. I never seen 'em walk. Cubby lays down to get a closer look. He can hear better'n me, but I don't think he can see better. What's real interesting is when one ant meet another ant going the other way they stop and it's like they're talking. Then they go on the way they were going. Wonder where they're headed. They kinda get lost in the leaves. I think I'll get my magnifying glass.

Suddenly Cubby's ears go up and he looks down the road and then he takes off. "Cubby! Cubby, wait! Come back here! Gosh darn, I wish you wouldn't chase cars."

"Hi, Mr. Crosby."

"Hi, Orvie. Your dog's quite vicious."

"Not really. He just likes to chase cars."

"Oh, I know. The first few times he rushed out at me I was afraid I would hit him and he kind of startled me, but I'm used to him now. How are you today?"

"Good. Did we get the *Saturday Evening Post*?"

"Yep, right on schedule. You like the cartoons?"

"Yeah, but right now me an' Mom are reading a Clarence Budington Kelland mystery. I can't wait to see what happens next. I hate ta hafta wait."

"Well, then, you better get to it."

"Thanks, Mr. Crosby."

I don't tell him I like *Tugboat Annie* too, which is another serial. I just wish they would put the whole story in one magazine because I hate to wait and they always stop right where it's an exciting part.

I usually get more mail because I send postcards to places all over. At first I cut out coupons from magazines, mostly *Holiday* magazine, and paste them on penny postcards. I put their address on the front and fill in my address where it says to, and they send me books and pictures and stuff about their beautiful places. I get 'em from a lot of national parks out west, like Rocky Mountain and Yellowstone with geysers. I got one from New York State with a picture of Niagara Falls. I'm gonna try to get something from every state an' from Mexico and Canada too. I already got one from British Columbia, which is in Canada, an' it has some really beautiful mountains with glaciers.

I start reading the Clarence Budington Kelland story right on the steps. Cubby looks kinda disgusted. He doesn't like it when I read.

Fishin' with Perry

"Mom, can I call Perry to go fishing?"

"I don't know. *Can* you? Do you know how?"

"I pick up the phone and when the operator asks me what number I say, 'Ring three.'"

"I guess you *can* ...."

"May I?"

"Yes, you may."

I pick up the phone and pretty soon the voice says, "Number please," and I say, "Ring three, please," which is Perry's number. She tells me to hang up, and pretty soon the phone rings three rings and then it rings three times again. Our number is 21, which is two long rings and one short ring. When it rings only one ring I pick up the phone 'cause I figured Mrs. Wick picked up their phone.

"Hello, Mrs. Wick. Is Perry there?"

"This you, Orvie? How are you today?"

"OK."

"Perry's outside; just a minute while I get him."

Jack an' Jill went up the hill....

"'Lo."

"Hi, Perry. Wanna go fishin'?"

"Ma, can I go fishin' with Orvie?" he hollers. "She wants ta know where."

"The bridge down by the Eversons.'"

"The bridge by Eversons.'"

Then his mom wants to know when.

"I got to get my hooks and some worms, an' then I'll head down."

"Pretty soon," Perry calls to his mother. "She wants to know when I'll be back."

"When we're done fishin', I guess."

"I don't know, a coupla hours ... She says OK."

"OK. See ya."

The Eversons' is about halfway to Perry's farm. It's not my favorite fishin' hole because there's trees and shrubs and branches on both sides of the brook, so the only place to fish, really, is from the bridge and even then a fish can take an' go under a branch and get the line tangled up. It didn't take long to get worms. There are loads of them around the compost piles. I'll probably beat Perry to the Eversons' bridge.

I keep meanin' ta ask Mom what that smooth grass like velvet is. Some of the Gabovitch's cows are drinking in the brook and just standing in the water chewing their cud. Ya know what cud is? It's grass and stuff the cows eat, but they don't chew it when they eat it the first time. It goes down in their stomach and when they have time to chew or if they just take the time they regurgitate (kinda like upchucking) a mouthful of the stuff in their stomach, which is called cud, and they chew it. If you haven't seen a cow chewing her cud the best I can do is to say it's like a person chewing gum. But I wish the cows were smart enough not to shit and pee in the water they drink, which is why I don't swim in the brook downstream from the pasture. Fishin' is OK though. I fish from this bridge by the Gabovitch's sometimes. I can't see any fish; the water's too muddy. Darn cows.

I like the road right here where it and the brook curve around the end of the hill, especially on a hot day like today, because there's trees on both sides and it's cool. There's no pasture on the hill 'cause it's steep and rocky. I can throw a stone in the brook from here. It's not far. Oops, hit a branch. Ah, splash. I like watching the ripples. Mr. Balack can't really use the land on this side of the brook for anything, and it just grows up brush and trees. I went swimming in the brook here once, but I don't go no more 'cause of the cows upstream and 'cause I was swimming next to a water moccasin, which is a poisonous snake with venom so strong one bite can kill ya.

The Eversons have a lot of fields where they grow corn and wheat mostly, and they have real interesting machines for harvesting. The brook cuts back across the road and heads off away from the road, and I don't know where it goes to after it goes through the Everson's fields.

I used to push the worm on the hook so it covered the whole hook, but even though the fish couldn't actually see the hook he could see the shape of the hook. 'Nother thing, if I left the worm on the hook for a few days it would dry out an' get hard, and it was hard to get off the hook 'less I soaked it in water first. Now I stick the hook through the worm's side then through the side again a little farther down, an' I do that a few times so you can't hardly know there is a hook there at all, just a squiggly worm.

"Hey, Orvie. Catch anything yet?"

"Naw. Had a couple nibbles."

Perry gets his hook caught on a branch under the water, and by the time we get it free both of us are wet up to our knees.

The brambles and bushes and just plain junk is hard to get through, but since we're already wet we figure we might as well wade downstream a piece where there might be a better fishing hole. We've never been down here before, but it comes out real nice with a corn field on one side and a wheat field on the other and, sure enough, as soon as we put our lines in the water we get bites. We both pull up sunfish right off and we put a stick through their gills and out their mouths and anchor the stick so the fish will be in the water but can't get away. We keep fishing, but it's as if the fish we caught were the only ones there and we're getting hungry, so I send Perry to find some dry wood for a fire and some sticks for roasting the fish while I clean them.

To clean fish you need a sharp knife; which my knife isn't all that sharp but it's OK. First, I hold the fish by the tail and scrape the knife toward the head to scrape the scales off. When I get the scales off I cut through the skin of the belly and open it up to get out the guts. This is where I wish my knife was sharper. Then I cut off the head and the tail and the spiny thing on the back, and I wash the fish in the brook.

Perry gets a campfire going right next to the brook where we can push it into the water to put it out when we're done. Now here is a good idea Perry has. He gets a couple of ears of corn and puts them right in the fire. Well, I want to tell you this is one of the best meals I ever ate—corn on the cob and fish about as fresh as ever there was. The corn is kinda tough, as it's field corn growed for the animals, but it still tastes great. I think cooking it on wood like that right in the husk is what made it better. Sunfish are pretty small, so we only have three or four bites of fish, but the smoke gives it a swell taste. If we had marshmallows it woulda been perfect.

We woulda gone back by the Eversons' farm road, which would've been a lot easier, but the Everson's ain't all that friend-ly, so we go back to the road along the brook. It's hard goin' through the brambles and all, but our sneakers and pants have mostly dried out. Bein' older I forge a path for us.

"See ya, Perry."

"See ya."

Boy howdy, the Gabovich's barn really smells today—not the barn but the pen where the cows wait to go in and get milked where the shit really piles up—an' it's worse 'cause it's wet. Our pig pen gets pretty smelly sometimes, but mostly we keep enough straw or old hay on the barn floors so they don't smell, and the hay and straw help make the compost better, too.

Henry's raking hay, but he doesn't see me when I wave. I guess the sun dried it out enough so he can rake it.

Zippity, doo dah, zippity a....

I wonder if *Holiday* magazine will come today. Maybe there'll be another picture to save, like the picture of the Cuban dancing girls twirling around with their legs showing all the way up to their panties.

"Hi, Mom."

"Orville, you look like you've been through the wringer!"

"What?"

"Look at you! Your face is scratched. Your sneakers and socks are caked with mud. Your pants are wet. You've got burrs in your hair and your shirt is torn. What happened to you?"

"Nothin. Just been fishin."

Won't...Wont...Wonet...Want

Spelling is really hard for me. The teacher says I'm lazy and that I should study more. We have the spelling test every Friday just before noon recess, an' if I get more'n five wrong I have to stay in and write each word twenty-five times. Writin' the words isn't so bad, 'cept I miss the beginning of recess so whatever everyone is playing, I'm just pretty much left out. Like if it's knock-up baseball, I just have to start out in right field, and recess is usually over before I get to pitch or bat.

One time Dad made me write "won't" as many times as it would fit on a big drawing pad, and I had to write regular size. There weren't lines on the paper and we were in his studio where he was working on some art for a cookie box and he looked over at me every so often an' if I was writing too big he told me to write small to make up for it or I'd have to do another page. It took more'n an hour and when I was done and he looked at it, turns out I'd got off track and there were actually four different spellings of it. He was really pissed, but he said he gave up on me and I didn't have to do it over again. I was glad I didn't have ta do it over again, but I was kinda surprised.

The good thing is I know how to spell it now, though sometimes I'll still get it wrong on the first try. I don't know what's wrong with me that I just can't spell. Instead of studying my spelling words now I just write all of them twenty-five times; that way if I get more'n five wrong, which I usually do, I can just give the teacher the pages I wrote at home and go right out to recess.

I Like Pretty Sunsets

I was practicing mumbly peg waiting for dinner. I'm pretty good at getting my knife to stick in the ground. I was practicing the one where I put the point of the knife on each finger and flip it off when Dad called me around in back.

"Orvie, come watch the sunset." He was sitting on the ground with his back against the apple tree. The sky was just turning orange. I sat on the ground between his legs and leaned back against him. "I love sunsets," he said.

"Do you love them as much as you love Mom?" He took a long time answering, which kinda worried me.

"Well, son," he said, "they're really different. With your mother there's a lot more going on. With a sunset you just watch it and think about how beautiful it is. Your mom's beautiful too but she's a lot more complicated than a sunset. You have to work at loving someone, but with a sunset, it's just there."

"Do you have to work at loving me?"

He laughed. "No, son."

"How come?"

The sun was behind a little cloud just about to set, and the colors were really exciting. There were sunbeams shooting out across the sky. I looked at Dad because he was taking even longer to answer this time. Maybe he was just speechless because of the sunset.

"That's a good question," he finally said, and then he was quiet some more. I was afraid Mom would call us in to supper before he answered. "When you were born you just peed whenever and wherever, and your mom and I had to change your diapers. We didn't get mad at you because that's what babies do. When you were old enough to walk we started teaching you to go to the bathroom or to pee outside. All that was work, but not the same as what your mom and I have to do to keep loving each other. I guess maybe we just accepted you as you were because you were a baby, and the same goes for now. Even though you can think and ask good questions, you're still not an adult and it's still our job to teach you things; but you're also your own person and we have to accept that. We may be able to teach you to not play with fire, but your interest in insects is a part of who you are and it would be foolish to try to change that."

"Do you want to change that?"

He laughed again. "No."

"Do you want to change things about Mom?"

"Yeah. That's where the work comes in."

"What do you want to change?"

"Oh, little things, stupid things really."

"Like what?"

"The way she sneezes."

"The way she sneezes?"

"Yeah, I'm afraid she'll blow her brains out the way she holds the sneeze in so it doesn't make any noise. It took me a long time to realize that that was just the way she sneezed and nothing I could say would change that. We used to argue about it."

"That's really stupid."

"I told you so. She used to hate it that I left my dirty clothes in a pile beside the bed when I got undressed at night. I put them in the hamper in the morning but that wasn't good enough. Finally she decided to let it go."

"But you put your clothes in the hamper before you go to bed. I seen you do it."

"*Have* seen. Yeah. When she stopped nagging me about it I decided to do it her way. It was a silly argument."

"It's on the table," Mom called to us.

Dad put his hand on my head as we walked into the house. The sun had set, the few clouds had pretty much gone away, and the sky was just reddish orange on the horizon. We stopped a minute, faced the sunset, and rolled our heads back. The color changed, getting paler—yellow, then green, then blue, and then dark blue, going almost black as night started to take over.

Are Chickens like People?

I think I told you before we have roosters with our chickens because we sell fertile eggs to a hospital in New York City for cancer research, but did I tell you how the eggs get fertile? First off, we don't have near as many roosters as chickens because it's not like they get married and there is one rooster for every hen.

I guess I better start at the beginning. Mr. Crosby brings us 100 chickens in a box. They are just little fluffy yellow chicks that hatched out the day before and they don't know nothing and they need to be kept warm, so we take 'em to the brooder house that Dad and me fixed up for 'em. In the middle is the brooder, which is a big round thing with a 'lectric heater so it's warm under there like if they were hatched under a broody chicken—that's a chicken that will sit on a bunch of eggs until they hatch and then she takes care of the babies showing 'em what to eat and drink an' when they are cold they go back under her to keep warm. The chicks we get never had a momma, so we got to take care of 'em. There are four waterers and four feeders around the brooder, so's any direction they go they can find food, which is mash we get at the feed store in 100-pound bags that have pretty prints that Mom can use to make clothes, though mostly Mom buys her clothes already made. But I think Mrs. Gabovich wears feed sack dresses.

When the chicks come Dad an' me take them into the brooder house and open the box and take out one chick at a time and dip its beak in the water 'cause they are too dumb to find the water without us doing that. Then we let 'em go and that's pretty much it. Usually they will just sit for a minute and then they will run. They don't ever seem to walk, just run, stop, an' run again. Oh, yeah, 'nother thing about the brooder house: we put up a circle of cardboard so they can't get too far from the brooder and not be able to find it, and it's in a circle so they can't get all bunched up in a corner and trample each other, which they will do 'cause they ain't... aren't... so bright.

I can tell which are roosters pretty soon 'cause they get bigger faster. When they get big enough to eat, we start eatin' 'em 'cause we only want about six roosters an' about half the chicks are boys.

So right now we got about fifty hens an' six roosters, so ya can see that the roosters have got a pretty good deal—'cept the ones we ate. You might think that a rooster just jumps on a hen whenever he feels like it, but that's not it. You'll see a rooster strutting around looking like he is the best thing since baled hay. The hens are just wandering around scratching and eating bugs and stuff and not paying any attention to him, an' then he'll chase a chicken and jump on her back, and when he's done he just gets off and she kinda shakes and ruffles her feathers and then goes back to scratching around for stuff to eat. Now this is the part I think is most interesting. I'm pretty sure the hen started the whole thing, at least some of the time. I seen a rooster just kinda minding his own business and a hen'll come around and kinda let him know she wants it. She don't go up to him and say, "Give it to me," but I'm pretty sure that's what's goin' on in her head. An' he'll just not pay attention at first, and then he'll get the idea she wants it and he'll like put one wing down and start going around in circles, and she'll be pretending she doesn't know what's what and then he'll go for her.

This is what makes me laugh, because when he tries to jump her maybe she just squats down and they do it, or maybe she will play hard to get and run away with him right behind her and then all of a sudden she stops and squats down. Ya know she could get away if she really wanted. She's not runnin' fast as she can, plus she could fly if she really don't want that ol' rooster jumpin' on her back.

We went shopping this Saturday like we always do, but Mom wasn't feeling good, so she didn't come and I had to help with the shopping instead of looking at the model trains in the model store window and getting a éclair at the bakery. In the summer I get a triple scoop ice cream cone at the newspaper store, but Dad didn't even give me a dime like he usually does.

When we were coming home I got to wondering if the hens always got laid by the same rooster, so I asked Dad.

"What do you think?" He's always trying to get me to think when I just want to know what he thinks.

"I think they do. They keep doing other things the same every day."

"What do you mean?"

"Well, there are three chickens that hang out under the pear tree most of the time."

"Are you sure it's always the same ones?"

"I'm not sure for sure, 'cause all of the chickens look pretty much the same, but I think so and there are five chickens that give themselves dust baths all the time; other chickens take dust baths too, but I think there are five that would get all wrinkled up if it was a real bath."

"Have you checked their numbers?"

"Ha ha. I'm not a rooster. They don't stop running when I try to catch them. Do you notice that the chickens usually lay eggs in the same nest every time?"

"They do?"

"Seems that way to me."

"Well, you would know. You collect eggs more often than I do."

"How come the rooster doesn't have sex with just one hen like people do?"

"Not all men have sex with just one woman."

"They don't?"

"No. Sultans have harems with lots of wives; Mormons can have more than one wife, too. I'm glad I don't have to feed any more roosters though."

"So the chicken house is a harem?"

"I suppose you could say that."

I think I am going to be thinking about that for a while.

Getting in the Hay

Dad had to work in the city today, which he hated because the hay was dry and ready to bring in. As soon as he got home he changed into work clothes and we headed for the Jeep. All the other farms have tractors and balers and wagons, but all we have is the Jeep, a sickle-bar mower, and a rake that we pull behind the Jeep. Our mower and rake are old fashioned—made to be pulled by horses. It takes two people, one driving the Jeep and the other sitting on the mower or rake to work the handles. There's a handle the person riding on the mower can pull that stops the blades from moving, and there's another handle to raise the bar. Mom drives the Jeep and Dad sits on the mower. The mower is real dangerous. When the wheels are turning, it makes the blades shuffle back and forth between the teeth. It'll cut your finger right off if you're stupid enough to put it in there. Sometimes a cat follows the mower because mice get scared and start running. One time our black-and-white cat was going along behind the blade and saw a mouse start running. She jumped over the blade to catch it and before Dad could stop the blades the mower cut off three of her legs. On any of the other farms she would have been put out of her misery, but we nursed her and she actually lived for years. A one-legged cat is not pretty, but I still loved her and fed her and petted her.

After the hay is cut it's left for a day or two to dry and then raked into windrows where it dries some more. The rake we have is called a dump rake, where the person riding on it lets the rake down with a handle and then, when the right amount of hay is in the rake, he pulls the handle that lifts the rake and dumps the hay. The idea is to go up and down the field, always dumping the hay in the same places so there are rows of hay. The other farmers then use a baler to pick up the hay, which is the easiest way, but we don't have a baler so Dad gets me set up in the Jeep with the seat all the way forward and a pillow behind me so I can reach the pedals. He has it in super-low gear, and I just steer along beside a windrow while he pitches the hay onto the Jeep. I push in the clutch if he wants me to stop. Mom would do this 'cept she's fixin' dinner. When it's loaded he drives it into the barn and pitches the hay up into the loft. I go up in the loft and pitch it farther back.

We're only about half finished and the Jeep is about half full with our tenth load when he tells me to stop, turn off the engine, and get out. I think I done something wrong, but he's just standing there looking up at the sky. It's purple with streaks of red and orange, all purple and red and orange, but mostly purple from west to east, the whole sky.

"This is a western sky."

"Whaddya mean, Dad?"

"It reminds me of the first sunset I saw in North Dakota. The whole sky was lit up like this, but the sky was much bigger."

"How could the sky be bigger?"

"The Dakotas and the states in the Midwest are mostly flat and planted with corn or wheat; there aren't many trees and no hills like ours to get in the way of the sky. The nickname for Montana is "Big Sky Country."

We just stand there for several minutes looking. Then we get back to work.

Corn

I'm pretty friendly with the Webbers, chicken farmers who live next door. Whenever Mrs. Webber bakes cookies or cake or something she gives me some, and Mr. Webber lets me ride on the tractor with him. Sometimes I help them with the eggs.

I like to help Mr. Webber take the corn off the cob with a neat machine he has. You turn a crank and drop the corn in a hole on the top. There are big metal wheels that tear the corn off the cob as it goes through, and the corn falls into a pail underneath and the cob shoots out a hole in the side. Farmers before this machine was invented must have had it really tough because it's not easy to get the corn off the cob with your hands. It's hard enough getting the husks off which the Webbers do when they pick the corn.

Sometimes I turn the crank and Mr. Webber drops the corn in the hole, but I like dropping the corn in best. I try to keep them going, so I have to be pretty fast picking up the ears and dropping them in the hole. If Mrs. Webber is helping out she has a second bucket ready, an' when one is full of corn she swaps 'em quick like. Then she dumps the corn in a sack that is hooked onto nails to hold it open. With all three of us working it can go pretty fast, and the corn cobs pile right up until they have to be shoveled to the side.

They put the bags in a bin that is supposed to keep the mice and rats out of it, but it don't always work. Every year Rudy, that's Mr. Webber's name, patches up holes with tin cans. They have lots of cats, which helps, too.

The corn kernels are too big for the chickens to eat, so before they feed them they run 'em through another crank machine that cracks the corn. Hannah, that's Mrs. Webber's name, cracks the corn and throws it on the floor of the chicken house where the chickens scratch around and eat it, which is why it's called scratch. They feed their chickens mash from the feed store too, but the scratch is cheaper and it gives the chickens something to do in the winter.

We have to buy scratch for our chickens in the winter when they can't go outside. I think we're the only farm on our road that doesn't have a tractor.

Tin Lizzy

Dad wants to go out west badder than anything. He says it is the most beautiful country in the world. Dad studied art after he got out of school, and he saw pictures of geysers and mountains and canyons out west that he said he just had to see, so he was able to save up some money and get some from Grandma an' got a friend who had a car to go out west with him. Dad says the car was a model T Ford, but he says everybody called it a "Tin Lizzy."

Back then cars broke down a lot, and he says it seemed like they had to patch tires just about every day because the roads were so rough. He says there were springs by each wheel to smooth out the ride and they broke both rear springs and one front spring on the trip and had to ride real slow until they could get new springs. Once, he says, they drove all day at ten miles an hour before they came to a garage that had a new spring.

He says the tires weren't so good either, and tires back then weren't much bigger than my bicycle tires. I've patched the tube in my bicycle tire and it's not really a fun thing to do. He says they had to have a pump and spare tubes and tube patches an' a spare fan belt an' oil an' they had canvas bags full of water hanging off the sides of the car, especially going across the desert, an' a can of gas in case they ran out of gas, which they did more than once. He says lots of gas stations had signs saying, "Last gas for so-and-so miles." He says one time they were climbing a mountain and ran out of gas, and when they put in the spare gas it just got them to the top an' they coasted down the mountain nine miles to where they found a gas station.

Where Does Instinct Come From?

"Orvie, wanna go hunting?"

"Come on, Dad, it's the middle of the summer—can't go huntin' in summer. 'Sides, what we going to use, the BB gun?"

"Don't need a gun. Come on, you'll see."

I was kidding Dad about the gun. I knew we were headed for the tomato patch cause this time of year when he comes home from work we hunt hornworms. If you haven't seen a hornworm, you'd be pretty amazed. You might even be scared because they are big, bigger than Dad's biggest finger. What'd even amaze you more is if I told you they were baby hummingbirds. You think I'm kiddin? Well, only kinda. These worms that can eat a whole tomato plant, tomatoes and all, are *Lepidoptera*. (You're probably wondering where I learned that word. Well, I'll tell you. Dad taught it to me.) *Lepidoptera* are sometimes butterflies or moths and sometimes worms, and in between they are chrysalises, which is like, well, like a mummy all wrapped up.

"Dad, do you tie the tomato plants to stakes so's it's easier to find the worms?"

"Not really, it keeps the tomatoes off the ground so crickets and wire worms won't get into them."

We have 12 tomato plants mostly tied up on stakes, but they aren't all on stakes. Some are kinda spread out on the ground. That hummingbird I was kidding you about is the moth of the hornworm, and it looks just like a hummingbird; in fact, it goes around from flower to flower just like a hummingbird and eats nectar. I've never seen two of 'em doin' it—actually I never seen moths of any kind actually doin' it—but they do, because the female moth lays eggs on the tomato plants, and that's how the worms get there.

Hornworms are hard to find because they are the same color as the tomato leaves and stems. Once you see one you say, "How'd I miss that?" They're pretty fancy with white stripes and a big old horn on their back end, but still, believe me, they are hard to see, which is why it's fun to look for 'em. I think they are the hardest to see of all the bugs. I don't know as I ever spotted one just right off without following the evidence—there are two things that make it easier to find 'em. One is their poop, which is like black or green round balls about the size of BBs when the worm is smaller and nearly the size of a marble when the worm is bigger, so you can kinda know what you're looking for size-wise by their poop. So that's one thing. The other is what they been eating. They eat whole leaves right down to the stems, and they eat green tomatoes. Sometimes a branch on the tomato plant is just stems—no leaves—and when you look down below and see all the dark green or black BBs you got a clue where to look. Trouble is they move around. I never find one just where I think it should be.

So Dad and me stick together checking out the same plant. I'll say, "Hey, Dad, there must be one here," and we'll start lookin' in the area where one's been eating. It's sorta like we're playing a game to see who can find the hornworm first. I remember when I was little I had some books where I was supposed to find stuff that was hidden in the picture. It's like that. If we've been looking for the same worm for a while one of us will say things like: "Come out, come out, wherever you are," or "Where's horny?"

We keep count of how many we get. I usually find more than Dad. He says I've got really good eyesight. Actually, what I've got is a little secret. I look for leaves that are just eaten a little bit, and sometimes the hornworm is on the underside of that leaf chomping away.

"Dad, if you had a choice between being a beetle or a butterfly, which would you want to be?"

"I don't know. A butterfly, I guess."

"Not me; I'd be a beetle."

"Why's that?"

"Take Japanese beetles. You always see 'em making love. My gosh, I've seen beetles waiting their turn. Seems like going at it is the only thing on their minds—that and eatin' just about everything."

Well, Dad just about split his sides laughing at that one. I think I'll tell it to the kids at school.

Japanese beetles are a lot easier to find than hornworms, as they are shiny black so it don't take any lookin'. They are also easy to kill. Just about all of 'em will drop off whatever they're eatin' when they think you're after 'em, so I put water in a tin can and hold it under the leaf they're on and then shake the leaf. Sometimes they start to fall just when they see my hand come near, which is why I have to make sure the can is in the right place.

I got ta thinking, how does a Japanese beetle know to drop when I shake the leaf, but when the wind shakes the leaf it just keeps on eatin' or fuckin' or both? I don't even have ta shake the leaf, just touch it, and they drop, which is a good way for 'em to get away if I'm gonna try squashing 'em, but what they don't know is I got a can of water under the leaf so they drop right inta that and are goners.

Some of 'em will fly right off the leaf without dropping, but most are pretty stupid and just drop right into my can. When I get so many they can stand on each other sometimes they will try to fly out, and that's when I take them over to the chickens and dump them out. The chickens love 'em. They come running from all over the chicken yard when they see me coming with a can in my hand.

I say Japanese beetles are stupid because they don't seem to have a lot of different ways to get away from me. It's like when they were deciding to play with me they didn't think about hiding or running—drop and fly and that's it.

Cucumber beetles got a lot more thought into how to avoid me. Maybe the Japanese beetles think that because they have a hard shell I can't hurt 'em, or maybe they weren't thinking about drowning or being fed to chickens, or maybe their plan is just to have so many that no matter what there would always be more coming, like Dad said the Japs did in the war. Maybe that's where they got their name.

Squash bugs only have one plan too: run like hell. I'm talking about the nymphs. I can understand them all being together in a group right after they hatch outta their eggs, 'cause the eggs are all close together, but they stay together mostly, and if they are on the underside of a leaf pretty soon the leaf will get a brown spot where they are eating. I don't know why, but I mostly squash them with my thumb. They are really soft, so it don't take much to squash 'em. Maybe that's why they are called squash bugs. Ha, ha, ha. That's a joke because they are called squash bugs because squash plants is what they like to eat. The adults are brown and 'bout an inch long, and are the first thing you find, usually under squash leaves that are lyin' on the ground, and usually there are two of 'em attached to each other, back end to back end. And lots of times a third one is just hanging around, left out of the fun, I guess. They don't move too fast so it's not too hard to catch 'em.

Their eggs are shiny brown and easy to see, but we don't look for them too hard 'cause they don't eat so much an' they're easier to spot an' kill once they start eatin'. I do scrape off any eggs I see when I'm looking for cucumber beetles, but I don't take a lot of time about it. When the eggs hatch, the little bugs are funny looking, kinda like spiders on stilts. The interesting thing is when they see me they run in all different directions, which is a pretty good plan, I think, and they do this right out of the egg. Now, come on, how did they get that smart right as babies? Would a baby person know to do that? I don't think so. It's like they see me and they start shouting to each other, "Run, run, it's the thumb! The thumb is coming!"

We finish up with the hornworms just in time, as Mom is hollering for us to come eat.

Friends

There are only two other kids who live on my road: Steve lives two farms up and Perry lives two more farms past Steve. Steve is older'n me. His father is a tomato farmer. They have a coupla cows and a garden and some chickens and pigs like us. We don't have cows. We have goats instead, and we have more chickens than they do, but they have a big field of tomatoes.

Steve taught me how to trap. He has a big trap line, about 50 traps I think. In the winter he gets up and goes to every trap before school. Mostly he traps muskrats, which he gets pretty good money for for their pelts. He skins 'em and then nails the skins flat to a board so's they don't shrink up when they dry.

Muskrat holes are in the banks of the streams, actually underwater. Ya have ta set the trap in the mud just right inside the hole so's they have to step in it when they come out, which in the winter is really cold work 'cause you gotta stick your hands in the water with the trap open and the trap has to be chained to something that won't pull out, like a rock or a tree root sticking out of the stream bank or something. Steve says he never got his hand caught in a trap, and I didn't either, but I was always afraid I would.

I only had three traps, and the only thing I ever caught was a skunk. Boy, what a mess. I had a really long pole that I tried to club it to death with, but the pole was too springy. I'd hold it up high and aim for the head and bring it down as hard as I could, but it wouldn't be a very hard hit. I didn't have any way to kill it, and I sure wasn't going to go up to it. I would have asked Steve what to do but I was ashamed, so I just left it there. I felt really bad but I didn't know what else to do. I didn't trap any more after that.

Steve is in high school. He wouldn't wanna hang out with me anyway, and besides he has to work for his father pretty much all summer. When the tomatoes get ripe his father hires me and some other people to pick 'em. I'm the youngest. Perry is too young. Everybody else is in high school. We get paid by the bushel basket. The hardest part of the job is moving the basket down the rows and then carrying the full baskets to the end of the row and putting it on the truck. None of us wear shirts. If you look out across the field, you'd just see our brown backs bent over the rows picking as fast as we can to make good money. When we grab a rotten tomato by mistake and have that squishy thing in our hand, you gotta know we're going to toss it in the direction of one of the other pickers, who is going to toss one back as soon as we're not looking. End of the day, we're all covered in tomato juice and seeds and smell like rotten tomatoes. Itchy? Oh, boy! We can't wait to get home and wash off, I'll tell you. Mom thinks it's hilarious because I'm not usually that interested in taking a bath.

One or two of us get to ride in the back of the truck to the train station to help unload. We unload them right into a boxcar. A man there counts the baskets and pays Steve's father.

The train comes along later and hitches onto the boxcar and takes them to the Campbell's soup factory in Camden, where they are made into soup.

Steve says he doesn't like working on the farm. He graduates from high school next year, and I guess he'll be heading off somewhere. I think he kinda wishes the war wasn't over so he could go fight the Germans or the Japs.

Perry is younger'n me. He's a nice kid, but we don't live all that close that we can really do much together. The most fun we ever had together was making forts with the bales of hay in his family's barn. We moved the bales around and made secret passageways and rooms that were really neat. We worked up there in the hay loft for days, and we had passageways all over the place and one room that we could almost stand up in. We had an emergency escape hole where we could drop straight down from the loft into a pile of hay. The neatest thing of all was a secret slide we made. We found this smooth board and we fixed the bales so it would hold the board so's we could slide down it.

Perry's dad got really mad at me when he smelled cigarettes on Perry. It wasn't because we were smoking in the barn, 'cause only a moron would do that, but he thought we were too young to smoke. He told my mom, but she didn't get too upset. Comes down to it, it was her cigarettes I was filching. I love the smell of the smoke and used to try to get near her when she smoked. When I have to take the trash out to burn I'll sneak one of her cigarettes and sit on the other side of the fire smokin'.

Perry and me did start a fire once. It was a windy day in the spring, and we were hangin' out by the brook when we decided to make a shelter from the wind. We gathered some sticks and propped them up to make a kinda lean-to and then we pulled dead grass and weeds and covered the sticks to stop the wind. It was really swell. We just sat there out of the wind feeling pretty smart. Then I got the not-too-bright idea to have a little fire right in front of the shelter. The little pile of grass I lit with a match caught right on fire. Trouble was the wind picked it up, and pretty soon the fire was heading off on its own. First we tried to put it out by stomping on it, but it spread fast. We ran into the brook, taking off our shirts while running, and dipped them in water and ran back to try to put out the fire, hollering for help. Mom came running with a blanket that she soaked in the brook and then Dad joined us. I tell you, we were really scared because if it got out of the field it would go into a thicket of brambles where we wouldn't have a chance of stopping it and then into the field on the hill and then into the woods at the top of the hill.

When we got the fire out all four of us flopped down on the ground. We were black with soot, sweaty and tired. After a bit, Dad got up and picked up the blankets and walked back to the house. I was afraid to move and so was Perry. When Mom finally caught her breath she looked at me, and I didn't know what was going to happen, but she looked almost like she wanted to hug me but she didn't.

"Perry, come on back to the house and we'll get you cleaned up," and we all headed back. I was sure I'd get a lickin', but I didn't.

Another Birthday

Mom and Dad seem disappointed that all I want for my birthday is penny postcards, but that's all I can think of. I got so many brochures they just about fill up the box I keep 'em in. I made dividers in the box for every state, an' I keep the brochures and booklets an' stuff arranged by state. Some of the best stuff is from Canada; I guess maybe Lake Louise is my favorite with the lake and mountains and glaciers an' all. I don't have all the states, an' Mom thinks if I send letters to the Chamber of Commerce in the capital of each state they might send me somethin', which I'm gonna do 'cause I want somethin' from every state.

I'm glad my birthday is tomorrow cause it's Sunday and Dad will be home, though if he went to work, he'd prob'ly bring some ice cream home.

"Somebody's comin'. It sounds like they're pullin' a trailer."

Mom comes out of the house to see an' Dad leans the fork he was using to turn compost and walks to the edge of the road, an' sure enough a rattly old truck with a trailer behind comes to where we can see it. Cubby is waitin' to attack it, but Mom tells me to put him in the house. I feel bad for Cubby 'bout that an' wish I hadn't said anything, 'cause he sure would've liked to scare that ol' truck. When it gets up next to Dad it stops and Dad tells him to pull it in by the barn. We all go to see what that was about.

I won't leave you in suspense any longer. The driver gets out and goes around to the back of the trailer and opens the door, and there's a big white horse and Mom and Dad say, "Happy Birthday!" So now I have a horse. Tell ya the truth, I don't really want a horse. I don't *not* want a horse. I hadn't ever thought about having a horse. Well, Dad did talk about a horse a little while back an' how it might be nice to have one, but I didn't pay no nevermind. There aren't any horses on our road.

The horse's name is Bessie, leastways that's what Jake (he's the man who drove the truck) says. Bessie has a halter on, which is how she was tied in the trailer. Jake leads her out and she takes a crap right as she's backing down the ramp an' we all laugh an' Dad says that would be a good addition to the compost pile. Bessie has a bridle, an' Jake shows us how to put the metal piece (it's called the bit) in her mouth and attach it so we can control her when we go riding, an' he shows us how to put on the saddle and to cinch it up tight so it don't slip around an' end up under the horse instead of on top, which, he says, would really be bad if someone was in the saddle. He says she sometimes will hold her breath to make us think the cinch is tight when it isn't, so we ought to tighten it up a second time when she's not expecting it.

Jake looks me up and down, an' then he adjusts the stirrups which is what ya put your feet in when you're riding. Then he tells me to come around to the left side of Bessie because ya always get on a horse on the left side. Don't ask me why, 'cause I asked and nobody seemed to know; it's just the way it is. Jake helps me get my left foot in the stirrup, which I couldn't quite reach standin' on one leg, an' Dad says he has a wood box that I can use to help me. Bessie snorts and moves a little an' I'm glad it's a western saddle, which means it has a horn on front ya can hold onto.

I won't bore ya with any more of this. I learned how ta use the reins by just laying them over to the direction ya want ta go; ya don't have to pull on 'em at all; an' I made her go by just nudging her with my heels and stop by pulling back on the reins and sayin', "Whoa, Bessie." That's all there is to it.

Dad adjusted the stirrups for his legs and took a ride. He'd rode a horse before a couple of times in Central Park. Mom wasn't interested.

After Jake left we rode around some more and then we put Bessie in the barn and gave her some feed and hay. I was beginnin' ta think this was a pretty good birthday present as Dad an' I stood there watching her eat. Then Dad said she was all mine an' that I was responsible for seeing that she was fed and got exercised every day and that her stall was cleaned out regular. He said I should ride her every day, except he would help out sometimes. I already had to feed and water Cubby, take kitchen scraps to the compost pile, burn the trash, an' keep my room picked up, but I didn't think it was a good time to remind Dad that I never said I wanted a horse.

Heaven

Perry's dog Seppy died. She was a nice old bitch. She was blind in one eye and couldn't see out of the other one. Ha, ha, ha. I guess it's not nice to make fun of her now that she's dead.

Perry is pretty sorry to lose her and I know what he means—I'd sure cry a lot if Cubby died—but he says she's in Heaven and that makes him feel good.

"What's Heaven like?" I ask.

"You don't know?" he says.

"No."

"Well, it's a wonderful place where you go when you die if you been good."

"Dogs go there?"

"People and dogs. My grandpa's there."

"How about cats?"

"Yeah, I guess."

"And frogs and fish?"

"I don't know. I don't think so. I don't think there's water there."

"What's it like?"

"It's where God lives, and Jesus and everybody who's been good."

"Sounds kinda crowded."

"It isn't like that. It's different than down here. It's just wonderful."

"What do you do there? Can't go fishin'. What's Seppy doin', ya think?"

"Seppy's prob'ly running after sticks and tryin' to catch butterflies."

"She can't see!"

"Oh, in heaven she got her eyesight back, and her legs are strong again. She can do everything. She can even talk."

Now that seems to me to be a stretch, but I decide to let it slide. "Is your grandfather chasing sticks, too?" I'm glad he laughed at that, 'cause it was kinda mean.

"No, he's waiting for Grandma."

"She gonna throw sticks for him?"

I don't know why but that gets us both going. We laugh so hard we cry and roll around on the ground and wrestle and I let him pin me. I tell him I'll take it back, and then we roll around and laugh some more. I'm still curious about Heaven. I ask him if there's grass there and he says he doesn't think so, and I ask if he thinks he'll get to go there and he says maybe but he'd have to be good, and then I ask if he thinks I'll would go there and he says he doesn't think so 'cause I don't go to church. So then I ask if somehow we both end up in Heaven would we still be friends and he allows as how we would, and then I ask if we'd be able to laugh and wrestle like this, and he thinks we would so then I say if there's no grass, that wouldn't be much fun, so he says maybe there is grass, but if there is, it won't ever grow long and have to be mowed. Now, I like that!

I ask Mom what she knows about Heaven, because she talks about going to church now and then, but Dad's always too busy on Sundays and besides he don't wanna make an extra trip into town that isn't necessary, and everything is closed on Sundays so no shopping or anything can be done. She says she doesn't know much about Heaven except that it's a wonderful place where we go when we die. I ask her what makes it so wonderful and she says it just is, which I tell her isn't a very good answer, so she says it's sparkly with diamonds and jewels and pretty things and there's no sickness. I ask if there's grass and she says she doesn't know, so I ask what people walk on because grass is the nicest thing to walk on barefoot or did everybody wear shoes. She's not sure but she thinks maybe everybody has wings and just kind of floats around or flies.

"Mom, you like to cook; would you be able to cook?"

"Oh, I don't think so. We don't have to eat in Heaven."

I'm not really stackin' up a lot of reasons to go to Heaven, I can tell ya.

"Are there fish in Heaven?" This was the make or break for me, because if I can't go fishing, I don't really see much point. I mean, floating around and flying sounds terrific, and I wish I could do that now, but just that would get pretty old. It would be great to fly to the fishing hole instead o' walkin', or, better yet, to float along over the brook looking for fish and just floating over a good spot and dropping the hook in, but if I had to choose between floating and fishing, no-siree, that's not for me.

"Mom, I'm going fishing."

I got this new place to fish where the brook goes right under the roots of this tree an' there's this mossy bank, that's what Mom said it was. This moss is like velvet. I really like sittin' on it, and I like to rub my hands over it. Say, I bet this is what Heaven is like; it's like grass that doesn't have to be mowed an' it feels good. It'd be fun to wrestle on this. 'Course we couldn't wrestle here 'cause it's too small a space an' we'd fall into the brook.

I been giving this Heaven thing a lot of thought. First, it don't seem like anyone knows what it's like except that it's wonderful. Second, people seem to make up what they think it's like, so I been thinkin' up my own Heaven. For sure it's got grass, and I like the idea it's always mowed grass like our lawn, or moss. The stubble in a mowed hay field is hard on the feet (and there won't be any thistles either, or ticks or mosquitoes). There will be streams and ponds and hills for sliding down, because I think hills are pretty, and trees, especially fruit trees and good climbing trees. And fish, lots of fish and worms and grasshoppers for bait … and a kitchen for Mom.

Mom an' Me Go to Church

I don't care much for churchgoin'. Mom likes to go, but the church she likes to go to is in town, which she would have to drive to and would cost gas money she doesn't want to spend. Besides, there's lots to do on the farm, so she doesn't really have time. Mostly I like that she doesn't go because she usually cooks a big dinner on Sundays.

She took me to the church in town on Easter. It's a nice church with big stained-glass windows. Mom said it was stained glass, but I can't figure out how you can stain glass, and it was all different colors and shapes, making up pictures of people in the Bible I guess.

In front of where we were sitting was a whole bunch of gold pipes standing on end, all different sizes, some of them as big around as our toilet vent pipe, and different lengths, too. Mom said they were organ pipes and that I'd hear the sound come out of 'em when the music started, and boy, did I! That music felt like it was inside of me vibrating my pipes and then a bunch of people came in and lined up right in front of the pipes and they waited a little while and then they started singing. It sounded nice and then everybody stood up and started singing the same song from books that were right in front of us. I took out a book and Mom handed me the one she was singing from and pointed to the place where the words were, but I don't really sing too good so I just kinda followed what they were singing in the book to see they got it right.

The minister got up and read from the Bible about Jesus getting killed and how his mother went to the grave and...no, wait, it wasn't his mother, it was another woman named Mary. I guess that was a pretty common name back then, and anyway he was gone from the grave. It was a pretty interesting story. Then they found him walking around, though they didn't recognize him at first, and I wondered what he was wearing, since the stuff he had been buried in was still in the grave and later Thomas, who said he wouldn't believe it until he saw it, did see Jesus and put his hand in the hole they poked in his side where blood and guts poured out. Anyway, after the minister read this story he sat down and the organ played and some men passed around trays with little glasses of grape juice, and other men passed around trays with little squares of white bread and Mom told me to hold the bread and juice. Then when everybody had some the preacher got up again and told us the grape juice was Jesus's blood and the bread was his body and we were supposed to drink his blood and eat his body, which didn't make me want to do it, but I did. Then there was some more singing and then the preacher got up and gave a speech about Jesus and going to Heaven and that Jesus was sitting on the right hand of God and that we could all go to Heaven because Jesus had showed us the way. Tell you the truth, I was pretty glad to get out of there.

On the way home Mom asked me how I liked it and I said it was OK. I didn't really like it except for the windows and girls and women dressed up in dresses and stockings and their hair all done up pretty. What I didn't like was that I had to get dressed up in a suit and tie. My grandma gave me the suit for my birthday and said it was my birthday suit, which got everybody laughing, and so it's always called my birthday suit, which is a joke because everybody says I'm in my birthday suit when I'm naked 'cause that's the way I was born.

Dad asked what I thought of church, and I told him the windows were awful pretty and I described the organ pipes, but I thought the rest was pretty boring. I told him I wasn't too happy about drinking Jesus's blood after Thomas had stuck his finger in it, which made him laugh. It seemed like he already knew the story. I asked him what he thought of Heaven and he said he didn't think much of it. He said he was busy enough worrying about this life to get involved with another one, which made sense to me.

I Learn Another Dirty Word

"Hey, Rollie!"

"What?"

I like Rollie, but sometimes he smells bad. He raises pigs and has even won a blue ribbon for one of his pigs. I think sometimes he can't get the smell of pig off o' him before he comes to school.

"I think there's a dirty word in our spelling book."

"Huh?"

"I think there's a dirty word in our spelling book. My grandma was helping me with my spelling an' all of a sudden she stopped and grabbed up the book and told me to wait right there. I couldn't figure out what I done wrong. She went right to the kitchen and started talkin' to my mom so I figured I'd better listen in. She said it was disgusting that there was such a word in the school spelling book. I guess she pointed to it for Mom to read 'cause she never said the word. She said Mom should go to the school board and have the book banned, that the school shouldn't be putting thoughts like that into our heads."

"What'd your mom say?"

"She said she'd look into it but she thought the word must have some other meaning and my grandma said she couldn't see what other meaning there might be. The good thing is she never came back to grill me on my spelling."

"What word was it?"

"I think it was 'intercourse,' 'cause that's where she stopped. Do you know what 'intercourse' means?"

"Nah. Eddie prob'ly knows. He knows a lot of that kind of stuff."

Eddie's dad is a judge and he's real smart, Eddie that is, not his dad, though I guess his dad is smart too. Eddie's playing catch with John K. (there are four Johns in our school) an' when we catch up with him John comes over to see what's up.

"Eddie, Orvie's grandmother thinks 'intercourse' is a dirty word an' shouldn't be in our spelling book. Do you know what it means?"

"Well, yeah, kinda. Sexual intercourse is a nice way of saying 'fucking,' which is what got your grandmother's knickers in a twist." I wish he wouldn't talk about my grandma that way but I don't say anything. "But sexual intercourse isn't the only kind of intercourse."

"What other kind might there be?"

"Well, I guess you could say we were engaged in intercourse right now."

"We?" All three of us say at once. That was a nasty thought.

"Not sexual intercourse, you dummies; just regular intercourse like we're talkin' to each other. If you don't believe me, go ask Mrs. Phillips."

I don't know about anybody else, but I'm not sayin' a word.

Church Again

Mom doesn't seem to wanna give up on the church thing, so a couple of weeks later she takes me to the church down by Mill Stream Crossing, which is only a couple o' miles away. It's not near as fancy. It doesn't have any colored windows or statues or organ pipes. The preacher just walks down the aisle from the back and steps up on a platform at the front and turns around and raises his arms and says, "All rise," and we all stand up, and he says "Let us pray," and then he starts praying while we stand there. They have song books like the other church and he tells us to go to a certain page and then he takes a harmonica out of his pocket and plays just one note and starts singing and so does everybody else. Then he reads some from the Bible and then an old guy gets up and plays the accordion, which sounds swell. Then the preacher gets all cranked up about Hell and how we will all go there unless we are good and righteous—I don't know what that means—and don't lie or cheat and are kind to others and don't abuse ourselves—I didn't understand "abuse ourselves" either—and help each other and don't sin. There seem to be a lot of things we aren't supposed to do. Then we all stand up to sing again, and after the song he prays for us again.

At the end the preacher is the first one out. I figure he's probably going fishing and wants to get a head start, but he's standing at the door shaking hands with everybody, and everybody is telling him what a good sermon he preached. He is especially glad to see Mom and me and makes a big fuss about seeing us and hopes he'll see us next week. I think Mom is a little hypocritical (that means saying something that isn't quite true, which I'm guessing is a sin) since she tells him it was a wonderful sermon and when he said he hoped he'd see us next week she said, "We'll see," which I'm pretty sure means, "Not likely."

On the way to the car I make a fool of myself by tripping and almost falling because I wasn't watching where I was going. I was watching Leslie Black and Suzie James, who were just standing there waiting for their parents, who were talking. They saw me trip and turned away and laughed, and I knew they were laughing at me. I'm glad they turned away because I could feel my ears get hot. I keep looking at them, though, because they look good from the back, too, in pretty dresses and all.

I asked Mom if we were going back next week. She asked me if I wanted to. It took me a while to answer because I was thinking about the accordion and Leslie and Suzie, but then I thought the rest of it was like cleaning out the whole chicken house just to eat one egg, so I asked her again if she wanted to go next week and, just as I thought she would, she said no. She said she didn't really like that kind of sermon but if I wanted to go she would take me, and I said I didn't want to go.

I thought the accordion was real interesting and I wished I had one to play. When I asked Dad if I could have one he said they were too expensive but if I learned to play the harmonica (it was in my Christmas stocking last year) he would see what he could do.

Just Dead

One o' the pigs died yesterday. I went out to feed 'em and there she was just lying there. The other two pigs were next to her nudging her to get up but she just lay there not movin' at all. We called the vet and it turns out she was shot. He figures it was a bullet from a hunter, probably from the woods at the top of the hill and wasn't actually shot at our pig but just hit her by accident. It didn't kill her right away, he says. He reckons it was probably in her for several days and poisoned her.

I asked Dad if he thought she had gone to Heaven. He allowed as how she was just dead. He was pretty darned angry at the stupid hunter and losing a pig he had bought and been feeding for a couple of months and now wouldn't give us any meat 'cause she'd been dead too long before we found her.

Exercising Bessie

I think Bessie'd just stand and eat all day if she could. She's not what you'd call a race horse type 'cause she has a really big belly. The door into the barn where we keep her is not very high, so I can't ride her out of the barn. I put on her saddle blanket an' saddle an' reins in the barn and then lead her out before I get on. Dad built a bench right outside the barn door, which I stand on to get on her. After I get her outside I give the cinch another pull and get her to stand next to the bench, which she doesn't really want to do because she is lazy, and she knows what's coming.

I don't mind exercising her all that much. Riding a horse is fun, but I think some horses might be more fun than Bessie. She really doesn't like going for a ride, and she especially doesn't like to trot or canter or gallop, leastways not when going away from the barn. I have to kick her in the ribs pretty hard most times to get her to go faster than a walk. She also tries to put her head down to eat grass so I got ta hold tight on the reins. I know I got ta show her who's boss, which I am, but I wish I didn't have to work so hard at it. I usually ride her up to the top of the hill, but I have to zig-zag across the slope as we go 'cause she don't like goin' straight up the hill. Every time I zig she tries to zag and go back down. She's kind of a pain in the ass that way.

At the top of the hill there's a path through the woods to an old road that some of the farmers use to get to their fields. Sometimes I go one way and other times I go the other way, an' I can get Bessie up to a gallop along there, but it's much easier to get her to gallop once I turn around. As a matter of fact it's as hard to get her to walk heading home as it is to get her to gallop going away. When she is gallopin' back I learned that the best thing to do when we get close to the path home is to pull like hell on the reins and holler, "Whoa! Whoa!" Cause I don't want to go down the hill too fast. No zig-zaggin' goin' down the hill, but I do get her to go on a diagonal with me holdin' her back. After it levels out I let her go charging straight for the barn.

I gotta tell you, the first time I rode her back to the barn at a gallop she almost killed me. I tried to get her to stop, but she went right into the barn and the top of the barn door knocked me off. I got a bloody nose and a bruise on my cheek. It's a good thing my feet slipped outta the stirrups when I hit or I would've really been hurt. It's really a lot of work to get her whoaed up before she goes into the barn, and I don't bother anymore. I just slip my feet out of the stirrups, and just as she is goin' into the barn I slip off her ass, which is kinda fun, like Hopalong Cassidy.

A Real Funny Story

Any time I say anything about Bessie not liking to exercise Dad tells me to stop complaining and how I need to let her know I'm the boss and all, so I stopped sayin' anything. Now this is the best story I've got. Dad took Bessie for a ride up the hill yesterday when he got home—he usually just rides around the fields so he can check on things while riding—anyway, he went up the hill and Bessie came back without him. I was worried at first but then I saw him walkin' outta the woods and I laughed to myself 'cause I 'uz pretty sure Bessie showed him who was boss. Sure enough his plan was to ride fast to the other end of the woods road, but Bessie's plan was to get back to the barn. When they got to the path through our woods Bessie turned for home and Dad kept goin' straight. I wanted to say something like, "Have a nice walk?" or, "The boss is in the barn waitin' to have her saddle taken off," but I figured keeping outta his way was a better plan. Makes me laugh every time I think of it, though.

Friends on Long Island

Dad's driving, Mom is in the passenger seat, and I'm in back. Riding in the back of the Jeep isn't all that much fun 'cause the canvas sides flap in the wind and the plastic windows are kinda yellow and scratched, so I can't see out all that good. There is a seat that is out most of the time as we're carrying feed or straw or something, but Dad put the seat in for me for the trip. I'm mostly leaning over the front seats so I can see out the windshield. We're going to visit Don and Jennifer Hick, who are artists too and have been friends from art classes before anybody got married. Mark is just about a month older than I am and he has a younger brother. They come out to the farm for a few days every summer, and we visit them about the same. This time I'm going to stay with them for a week, and they will bring me home.

"Roll up the windows." That's a joke, because rolling up the windows, if the Jeep had windows you could roll down, would not keep out the smell. Secaucus is the smelliest place on earth. I'm not kidding, you oughta have a gas mask to drive across the Pulaski Skyway, which is kinda a neat road without the smell as it goes up over all the pig shit and garbage that is making the smell, but it's not just pigs. There are smoke stacks with black smoke and yellow smoke and brown smoke and white smoke. I don't know how anybody can live there. I try to hold my breath but can't for near long enough, and then I hold my armpit up by my nose, which smells a lot better than the air.

When we come down off the Skyway we go into the Holland Tunnel, which goes under the Hudson River. It's the longest tunnel I've ever been in. Come to think of it, I guess it's the only tunnel I've been in. Mom gets all kinda weird, like she's gonna be sick or something. She's afraid the tunnel might collapse an' we'll drown.

The smell of exhaust fumes isn't half bad after Secaucus, and then we're in New York City, the biggest city in the world. And it's where Dad works. The rest of our trip is all city, tall buildings, then a bridge because New York City is on an island and our friends live on another island where there are houses with yards and all but no farms and no dirt roads; all the roads are pavement. The Hicks live in a nice house with a front and back yard, but it's kinda noisy because the approach to the Whitestone Bridge is just a stone's throw from their back yard.

It's funny that people would call us hicks for living on a farm when the real Hicks live in the city. When I was younger they took me to a midget car race. There were big stands and tons of people. I had to go to the bathroom real bad and I had to go by myself because nobody wanted to miss part of the race. The problem was I got lost and couldn't find my way back to my seat. I was just about to cry when a nice lady asked me if I was lost and took me to the place where they announce the races and they asked me my name and I told them and said that I was with the Hicks. Mr. Hick came and got me, and when I got back to my seat Mark was very, very mad at me because when the announcer said I was with the Hicks everyone laughed.

Mark takes me down in the cellar to his dad's shop to show me a model airplane he is making. The wings are about as long as my arm. It's made out of balsa wood, which is real light, but the wood is just to make the shape, like the wings have about ten pieces of wood glued to three pieces of wood that are the length of the wing, and they make the shape of the wing with the biggest being close to the plane body and each one gets smaller the farther out it goes. Then paper is stretched over the wing and painted with something that makes the paper get tight. The stuff he paints the wings with smells kinda like gas, only much better. It's called "dope." I really like the smell.

Then we take off for the river where there is a park with a playground and ball field. The bridge is right there going over part of the park, and it is really big.

When we get back to the house there is lots of food to eat and lots more people. They are mostly artists. The grown-ups have cocktails and are pretty funny. We have to get introduced to everybody and shake hands and all, and then we fill up some plates with food. Mark's mom is a real good cook, like my mom, and everyone is complimenting her on the curry that is a seasoning in pretty much everything. It's OK but I kinda hope my mom doesn't start cooking with it. We take our plates up to Mark's room, which is where I am going to sleep for the next week. He has two beds in his room.

We play Parcheesi and eat, and then we go back downstairs to get some dessert. It's getting pretty noisy. Mark's mom says we can't take the dessert upstairs so we watch the adults playing some kind of game that only one person knows how to play. They pass around a pair of scissors, and whoever's holding the scissors is supposed to say if they're crossed or uncrossed.

Sometimes the scissors are open and sometimes closed but that doesn't seem to matter. Sometimes people are right and sometimes they are wrong, then Dad starts getting it right every time and he can tell others if they're right or wrong. Well, it's pretty crazy and some people are getting pretty frustrated, so the man who knows how to play said Dad is the winner and he tells the others that crossed or open didn't have anything to do with the scissors except with who's holding the scissors. If the person holding the scissors has their legs crossed the right answer is "crossed," and if they aren't crossed the answer is "uncrossed."

After seconds on dessert, Mark and me go back upstairs and play games that are much better than that one, which is really any game ever.

We get up early in the morning because Mark has a paper route. There's a heavy bundle of newspapers on the sidewalk in front of their house, which we lug into the garage, and Mark shows me how to fold the papers. Ya fold both sides in toward the middle and push the side with all the pages into the side with the fold so the paper is one third the size. They all go into a canvas bag just so, and Mark slings it over his shoulder and gets on his bike. He can reach into the bag and pull out a paper while riding and throw the paper on people's porch without stopping. I have a bike they borrowed from a neighbor, which is a girl's bike and makes me feel a little bad. I just follow along the first couple of days, but then he lets me carry the bag a couple of times, and I get pretty good at throwing the papers, though he has to get some I miss.

We play catch and ride around the neighborhood on bikes, which I like a lot 'cause it's pretty flat and all smooth tar, which is a lot nicer to ride on than the dirt road at home. We could even ride to a store and get a soda or candy or something.

Mark shows me how to take the cork out of the soda cap and make the cap stick to my shirt like a pin or medal.

One day we all go over to the Hudson River where a friend of theirs has a boat and I guess I say something I shouldn't. We're standing on the dock, Mark, his mom, and me, and I'm lookin' at the water and I see all these white things floating around like some kind of fish or somethin' and I say, "What are those pretty white things?" and Mark and his mom kinda look like they're going to laugh and they turn away and act like they haven't heard me. I know I've said something wrong but I don't know what it is.

There are lots of boats, sailboats, and motorboats and some really big fancy boats. We're waiting for Mr. Hick and his friend to get the boat ready to go sailing. We 're going to sail under the George Washington Bridge, which is bigger than the Whitestone Bridge. It's the biggest bridge I ever saw. Sailing is OK, and it's neat sailing under the bridge, and we had sandwiches and soda and we saw the Palisades, which is a really high bank on the New Jersey side of the river. The river is between New Jersey, where I live, and New York, where Mark lives.

That night when we go to bed Mark tells me what the white things were. He says they were condoms, which are also called rubbers. I really feel like a dummy 'cause I didn't know what they were, and he tells me they're what men use to keep from having children, and he tells me a poem which I think is pretty funny. This is the poem:

> In days of old,
> When knights were bold,
> And rubbers weren't invented,

They tied a sock around their cock,
But children weren't prevented.

I'm going to have fun telling that one when I get back to
school, and I'm not going to feel so dumb.

In the Dark

Bill and Hortense are coming to stay with me while Mom an' Dad go to Uncle Orville's funeral. He's not my uncle, he's my dad's uncle and he has the same name as Dad and me. He is a real interesting person. He went west in the Gold Rush. I like to hear his stories about when he was out there climbing mountains, panning for gold, and working at lots of jobs, all kinds of jobs, like in stores, tending mules, an' going on pack trains into the mountains for months an' eating really pretty bad food.

He lives in Camden now. Well, I guess he doesn't *live* there anymore, but that is where we visited him. His house is on a street with a train track right down the middle, not like a trolley track but a real train track with big, long freight trains and passenger trains going right by his window. He was always sitting in a big chair in the window. Actually, it was three windows that kind of stuck out from the house, so where he sat he could look up and down the street. He was retired from the railroad. That was his last job and he had it for a bunch of years, a lot longer than I've been alive.

Every time a train went by he'd take his watch out of his pocket and say if the train was early or late or on time, like, "Seventy-four is two minutes late; she's always just a couple

141

of minutes late." He even knew the engineers on some of the trains, and sometimes they would wave at him or even give a little toot on the whistle. These were big trains, steam engines. They shook the house when they went by and left a cloud of smoke that settled on the street after. I loved to watch 'em with the steam puffing out from the pistons that drive the wheels. When we were visiting, Uncle Orville would call me when a train was going to come.

I think he has, eh, had, elephantiasis but I'm not sure. I think that's what I heard someone say, but, anyway, his ankles looked like a elephant's legs. They were really big. He hardly ever left his chair except to go to bed, which the last time I saw him was right near his chair.

Anyway, he died and Mom and Dad are going to his funeral and Bill and Hortense are coming to stay with me. They're nice. They don't have any children. Hortense is an artist, which is how we know them. She makes little ceramic things, mostly animals. They live in Greenwich Village, where Hortense has her kiln—a kiln is like a oven—where she bakes her pottery. She usually brings one or two little animals when she comes for a visit. She gave me two little cats that look just like my cats. I don't know what Bill does. When they visit, he pretty much just sits and reads.

Mom and Dad should have been back by now. Something is going on but I don't know what's happening. There've been some phone calls, but Hortense talks soft and I can't understand what she's sayin'. I ask why Mom and Dad aren't back yet, and Hortense says they got delayed, and then she says they are staying in Philadelphia for a while.

It's been a week since Mom and Dad went to the funeral. Hortense went to town with Rudy when he was delivering eggs, an' she went shopping an' brought back a bunch of groceries.

Bill read the *Reader's Digest* straight through from page one without skipping around. You'd think he would complete one story like I do. When I read "Tug Boat Annie" in the *Post* and it says, "Continued on page whatever," I go to that page to keep reading the same story, but Bill just reads straight through. That's got to be confusing. I don't know how he can keep track of it.

I'm gettin' real worried about Mom and Dad. I don't sleep too good. I'm beginning to be afraid they won't ever come back.

In Greenwich Village, where Bill and Hortense live and Hortense has her kiln in their apartment on the first floor, they have a window on the street. Hortense puts her ceramic animals on glass shelves in the window so people walking by can see them, ring the bell and come in and buy them. I think she is worried about being away so long.

"Are Mom and Dad coming home today?"

Bill and Hortense have their bags packed and are putting them by the door, so I guess it's a stupid question. About time, I think. I mean, I like Bill and Hortense OK, and they played games with me whenever I asked them, checkers mostly, and Hortense made lots of cake and cookies and stuff, but I miss my Mom and Dad.

"Your grandparents are coming."

"I thought Mom and Dad were staying with them."

"They'll tell you all about it."

Now I know something is wrong. I don't know what to do. Cubby is sleeping by the fireplace, so I just lie down next to him with my arms around him and he kinda snuggles up with me. We stare right at each other and he cocks his head a little to the side, which is what he does when he is asking a question, and then he licks my cheek. I didn't even know I was crying. I think we both know something is very wrong.

We hear a car and Cubby and me run to see who's coming. It's a taxi with Grandma and Grandpa, and when it stops I run and ask them where Mom and Dad are. Grandma wants to hug me, but I just want to know what's going on, and she says they're fine.

"Well if they're fine, why aren't they here?"

Hortense and Bill are loading their bags into the taxi, and Bill carries Grandma and Grandpa's bags in the house, and it's all pretty confusing with everybody telling everybody what they need to know except nobody telling me nothing. An' then we wave good-bye to the taxi an' then we have to go in the house and Grandma makes me sit down on the sofa an' she sits next to me and Grandpa goes out on the porch to smoke his pipe and Grandma puts her arms around me an' by now I figure I'm an orphan.

It turns out Mom and Dad had a accident an' the Jeep flipped over and Mom was thrown clear and Dad was trapped under it until they could lift it off of him. They're in a hospital and Dad will be home tomorrow. Mom is OK but has to stay in the hospital for a couple of more days.

I don't want to sit on the sofa anymore. I'm kinda angry. What do they think I am, a baby? I almost wish I was a orphan, at least I wouldn't have to go through that again. I go outside and sit near grandpa where I can smell his pipe.

I Learn to Cook

"Dad's comin'!" I shout at the house. Cubby and me've been waitin' for him and, of course, we recognize the sound of the Jeep before we can see it. Grandma and Grandpa come out on the porch and we watch the road in front of the Webbers' for the first sight of the Jeep coming up the hill, but we're surprised that the first thing we see is Dad's head. There's no windshield or top on the Jeep. Cubby and me run up when he stops and, boy, Dad's face looks real bad. It's all purple around his eyes, he has a bandage on his head, and his nose is bandaged, too.

"Dad, how'd it happen?"

Now that I know Mom and Dad are OK it's kinda exciting thinking about rolling over. Dad scratches Cubby's head and then he puts his hand on my shoulder kinda leaning on me while he swings his legs outta the Jeep. He gets out slow and it kinda takes him a little while to get standing up straight. Then Grandma comes up and hugs him without squeezing too hard.

"How'd it happen, Dad?"

The Jeep doesn't look as bad as Dad. The top and the bars that held it up and the doors are all just kinda mixed up in the back, and there's no windshield so it looks like it does when we take in hay and we fold down the windshield on the hood 'cept

145

it isn't on the hood. I look the Jeep all over and there isn't hardly a dent in it. There are some scratches and some dirty places but that's all.

He and Grandpa and Grandma head for the house. He's holding his backside and kinda bent over some. I ask him again what happened and he says there was oil on the road on a curve and the Jeep skidded and rolled over and that was all.

He calls Norm who he bought the Jeep from and Norm says he'll have a new windshield in a couple of days, and Dad thinks he can fix the rest of it, but the way it is he can't really take Grandma and Grandpa to the bus to go home, so Mr. Webber takes them.

Dad and me eat mostly eggs for a couple of days. He says Mom is coming home today so Cubby and me are sittin' on the stone steps waitin' for her. Her mom, Grandma K., is bringing her in Aunt Hat's car. Dad says it won't be till afternoon but we're not takin' any chances, an' sure enough it's not noon yet an' we hear a strange car. I put my hand on Cubby's collar, not holdin' it or anything, an' he knows this is a special car and not to chase it, an' along comes Aunt Hat's big black car with no-body driving it! Ha, ha. Grandma's lookin' out under the steering wheel and Mom's in the back seat. I don't guess I've ever been happier to see somebody. We run up to the car as soon as it stops an' I open the back door and give Mom a big hug. Cubby just sits waggin' his tail.

Mom doesn't look bad at all, not like Dad, but one leg is up on the seat out straight with a big cast on it. Jimmy V. had a cast on his arm once from fallin' outta a tree and we all signed our names on it and wrote funny stuff and drew pictures. I give

Grandma a hug when she gets outta the car. I'm bigger'n she is now. Dad comes out an' helps Mom outta the car and gets her on her crutches. I'm hoping Mom will let me try out the crutches 'cause they look like fun.

The Jeep got fixed and Dad is working in the city again, but Mom can't get around too good so I'm learning how to cook. She sits in a chair and just tells me what to do and where things are. It's not really all that hard. We mostly have meat and potatoes and a vegetable. There's two ways to cook potatoes: quickest is to cut 'em up and put 'em in water and boil 'em, but I like baking 'em better 'cause I don't really have to do anything but turn on the oven an put the whole potatoes right in there and set the timer for an hour. Vegetables are pretty much the same as boiling potatoes except what I have to do before putting 'em in the pot. String beans I have to snap off the top and pull the string off o' the bean, carrots I have to peel, and broccoli I have to look for the worms and cut it up in pieces. I already know how to take the string off the beans 'cause I did that before when I helped Mom can them. Sometimes we have succotash, which is corn and lima beans in a package from the freezer. We wouldn't usually have frozen succotash in the summer, but with the accident an' all the garden isn't in such good shape. Mom sends me out there to try to find something to eat an' I mess around in the weeds and can usually find some stuff, but sometimes I tell her I can't find anything good 'cause I kinda like succotash, an' the frozen peas are pretty good, too.

I'm roasting a rooster. Dad killed it, took off the feathers, and gutted it this morning after breakfast. I'm kinda excited 'cause I don't want to make any mistakes. Mom told me to start the oven and set it at 375 degrees, an' then she told me to shake on lots of salt and pepper and rub butter all over it, which was real messy. This is a real special treat because it is the first rooster we're eating from a new flock of chickens. We get what's called straight run, which means hens and roosters, and when the roosters are big enough to eat we eat most of 'em. When the birds are older they get awful chewy. Mom cans them in the pressure cooker, which she is kinda scared it will blow up, but the chicken is real good.

Mom taught me how to make meatloaf and macaroni and cheese, which are good to make because they last for three days when I don't have to cook. I'm sure gonna be glad when Mom gets that cast off her leg. She said the accident happened because Dad was driving too fast in the rain. She asked him to slow down but he didn't and lost control of the Jeep on a corner. Maybe she didn't see the oil slick.

Rethinking Church

I had a nightmare about Hell, about everybody screaming and burning and drowning and choking and gasping for breath and snakes and bugs and everybody trying to get out but ugly men kept pushing us back in with pitchforks. I woke up and Mom was there. She said I was screaming and I was all tangled up in my blankets with my pillow over my head. I kept thinking about Hell. I was afraid I would go there and I didn't know what to do.

I was over to Perry's and we were just kinda fooling around on the tractor and I figured he might know something about Hell. He goes to Sunday school every week while his parents go to church and sometimes he goes to church, so he knows a lot more about all that than I do, so I asked him what people were supposed to do to keep from going to Hell.

He tells me, "You mustn't lie, or cheat or steal or say bad things about people or jerk off or…."

"Jerk off?" I shout. "They told you in church you'll go to Hell if you jerk off?"

"Nah, my dad told me that." Perry jumps off the tractor wheel and sits in the shade. I lean over and look down at him.

"What made him tell you that?"

"I think my mom told him I was doing it." I jump down and we both sit leaning back against the wheel.

"How'd she know?"

"Oh, well, she kinda caught me. She pretended she didn't but that night my dad talked to me about it."

"So you're going to Hell because you jerked off?"

"No, only if I do it again."

"So if I stop jerking off, I won't go to Hell?"

"I don't know. I think you have to go to church too and have to confess your sin."

"What's that, confess?"

"You go into the confessional, it's like a phone booth only no windows, and the priest slides open a little window like except you can't see him through it and he asks if you have anything to confess." Perry is picking the petals off a daisy and I'm just staring at him.

"And you tell him you jerked off?"

"Ya say, 'Bless me father for I have sinned,' and then he asks me what I done and I say I masturbated."

"You what?"

"Masturbated. That's the proper word for jerking off."

Master bait. Sounds like something to go fishing with. "Then what?"

"He told me not to do it again because God doesn't like it and that I should pray every night for the strength to not do it."

"How's that goin'?"

"Not so good."

"So every Sunday you confess?"

"Naw, I only have to confess once a year unless I do something really bad."

I get back on the tractor and lean my elbows on the steering wheel. I can't imagine not jerking off so I s'pose maybe I ought to go to church just so's I can jerk off without going to Hell.

I Commit a Terrible Sin an' Almost Die

When I got up yesterday morning there was a big red mark on my chest on the right side. Mom took my temperature and that was normal, she said, then she called the doctor, who didn't seem to be very helpful.

It seemed to go away pretty much by the time I went to bed, but then this morning that place was OK though it still itched some but there was another place. Mom called it a splotch about the size of her hand when she called the doctor this time, and he came out to the farm to take a look.

He says it's hives and there isn't anything that can be done about it, but it will just go away pretty soon. Mom asks him what caused it and he says nobody really knows but he thinks it might be caused by worry in some people.

"You aren't worried about anything, are you, Orvie?" Mom asks.

"No, ma'am."

Mom gives me a hard look. I don't know why I called her "ma'am," and it sure raised her eyebrows. I hate to lie to her but I don't want to break my promise to Mr. Webber so it just seems like I'm stuck.

Day before yesterday I was riding on the back of Mr. Webber's tractor, which I really like to do. He and Mrs. Webber don't have any kids of their own so they kinda make me feel special and let me do things and give me cookies, and they have a television, the only one on our road, and they let me watch it any time I want, which isn't very much, only at night and I have to get permission, which isn't too easy to get 'cause Dad don't think I should watch it. He thinks it'll hurt my eyes and that there isn't anything good to watch anyway, same as he won't let me listen to radio shows Sunday afternoon when *The Shadow* and *Amos and Andy* and *Nick Carter, Master Detective* and *Edgar Bergen and Charlie McCarthy* are on. Once I hid the radio under the firewood next to the fireplace an' lay down real close to it. I almost got caught when I laughed out loud at Charlie Mc-Carthy. I pretended I was laughing at a cartoon in the *Saturday Evening Post* that I was pretending to read.

So anyway, there I was riding on Mr. Webber's...Mom and Dad call them Rudy and Hannah, but out of respect I call them Mr. and Mrs. Webber...anyway, I was sitting on the platform Mr. Webber built on the tow bar of his tractor. I stand on that and hold on to the back of his seat when he's going fast. Well, this time I was sitting on the platform and dragging my feet and the grass and weeds were tickling my feet and it felt neat, especially when big flowers like daisies and dandelions hit the back of my legs.

He had a load of manure on the manure spreader. He has lots of manure, mostly from the chickens. He and Hannah have a chicken farm and they have some pigs and a calf that's gonna be hamburger, but they mostly make their money selling eggs. Sometimes I ride with Rudy in his car when he takes the eggs to market, which is about every day. He can only fit four cases of eggs in the back of his car with the seat out. Each case is pretty heavy and has 30 dozen eggs in it.

Well, anyway, I was sitting on the back of the tractor dragging my feet and watchin' the shit fly when Rudy turned at the end of the field and the front wheel of the manure spreader came close to the tractor. I wasn't watching and it ran over my foot, which caused my foot to stop moving while the tractor kept going, which pulled me off the tractor. The wheel only ran over my foot, but I was under the whole manure spreader and the spinning blades that throw the shit all over the place were comin' at me. Rudy heard me hollerin' and stopped the tractor just before the blades got to me. It was very scary and I guess he was real scared, too, because he jumped off the tractor and ran back, and when I crawled out from under the spreader he was white as a ghost.

He looked at my foot and felt it and moved it around and I said it was fine and didn't hurt at all, which it didn't. I felt fine, only a little scared. Rudy asked me to promise not to tell my parents, which I didn't really understand 'cause it was my fault so why should he worry about it, but I said OK because I was afraid if Mom and Dad, Mom especially, heard about my close call with death they might not let me help Rudy anymore.

That might have been the first time I lied to my mother. I didn't like it much and I think that was why I got the hives, and hives were scary and didn't feel good. I kinda felt like maybe that was a sample of Hell.

Guys Don't Sew

"Orvie, stop right there, please. Would you please collect the eggs before you get out of your wet clothes?"

Mom takes my books from me and gives me the egg basket. I can tell by the smell that she has something good in the oven. She always has something for me to eat when I get home from school, usually carrots or an apple but I think she is making cookies. It's raining cats and dogs, but I'm not really wet 'cause of my poncho. There are a lot of chickens in the nests, which Mom should've let them out before this, but it's not so much a problem if they have to hang out in the nests for a couple hours. They prob'ly don't even mind when it's raining like this.

"Thanks, honey. Leave your poncho and boots by the door. How was school today?"

"OK."

"What did you learn today?" She's expecting me to say "not much," which is what I usually say, so she was surprised when I told her we sewed a flag.

"Sewed a flag?"

"What smells so good?"

"Oatmeal and raisin cookies. You can have two when they cool a bit. Tell me about this flag."

155

"Teacher had a big blue cloth she spread out on the table by the windows. It had white circles in the center like a bullseye, and we had to take turns sewing on white pieces and talking about the United Nations. The center was supposed to be the North Pole, an' there were white patches for the continents, and on the flag there were gray outlines of each continent and we were supposed to match up the patches and the outlines and sew the patches in the right place; and then around the circles we had to sew on a wreath of leaves like, and they were supposed to be olive branches because olive branches are a symbol of peace. I thought it was kinda dumb."

"Dumb? Why?"

"I don't know; guys aren't supposed to sew. The girls were kinda laughing about it."

"What did you learn about the United Nations?"

"They're gonna build a big building for it in New York City and the land and all are not going to be part of the United States anymore. It's gonna be international, like a country except that it's no country. May I have a cookie now?"

"I 'spect they're cool enough now. What are they going to do in the United Nations?"

"Make sure there aren't any more wars."

"That would be nice."

Sears Catalog

"You get the Sears catalog at home?"

"Yeah, you?"

"Yeah. What's your favorite part?"

"Whaddya mean?"

Eddie and me are taking a leak at the trough in the boys' outhouse.

"Do you jerk off?" Eddie asks me.

"Yeah. Oh, you mean to the pictures in the catalog? Yeah."

"What are your favorites?"

"Ladies' underwear; I especially like panties—and girdles."

"I like bathing suits."

"I like them too, especially tight ones, the ones that look kinda like a open bottom girdle."

"I like men in bathing suits and I like men's underwear," Eddie said. "Shake it more than twice and you're playing with yourself. Ha, ha."

"You like men's underwear?" I asked as I zipped up.

"Yeah."

I didn't know what to think about that. We headed out to the ball field.

Who Made Satan?

Perry and me are sitting on the bridge by Gabovich's fishin'. It's easy 'cause all ya have to do is drop the hook in the water and the current takes it downstream, and then ya just pull on the line every so often to make it more interesting for the fish. I got a cork on my line, which keeps the hook a little off the bottom. Perry's got a real bobber made outta red-and-white plastic. Whenever the cork or the bobber goes underwater we pull on our line and hope the fish took the hook. Sometimes the cork will just bob a little bit and if you pull you don't get anything 'cause the fish was just nibbling at the worm and hadn't got a good bite at it. I'm pretty good at knowing when the fish is just fooling around and when it's taken the hook.

Perry says that God is good and loves everybody and that he made the earth and everything, so I ask him if he made Hell and he says no, that Satan made Hell. Now, ya see, right off there's something wrong. If God made everything then he must have made Hell, or he didn't make everything. Take your pick. So then I think, God didn't make the brooder house. Dad and I built that, so it's OK that Satan made Hell, but when I ask Perry if God made Satan he says no again. So we're back to God didn't make everything.

Perry explains that Satan and God and some other angels were already around when God created Earth. I ask him what they were doing.

"I don't know. Like us, I guess, just sittin' around."

"What, were they just watching God create Earth, then?"

"I guess."

"So, then Satan says, 'I'm going to create Hell,' or what?"

"Yeah. I think he was jealous because God created this swell universe with animals and stars and people and everything and Satan couldn't do it so he made Hell."

"What were the angels doing? Do they ever come to Earth?"

"Sometimes, I think, to give God's messages and stuff."

"So they're messengers?"

"Yeah, pretty much, I think. I think they sing sometimes."

Perry gets a bite but the fish gets away. He pulls in the line and puts another worm on the hook and just then the same thing happens to me. As I put on a fresh worm I ask him what Satan does.

"Oh, he comes down to earth a lot. He is the one who tempts us to do wrong things because if he can get us to sin and we don't confess to the priest then Satan gets us and we go to Hell."

"Does God come down to earth?"

"No. He sent his son Jesus but he never came himself."

"Why not? Why doesn't he come down like Satan and tempt us to do the right thing?"

"I don't know."

"Seems like it'd be a good plan."

It starts getting hot, so we go under the bridge to get out of the sun.

Instinct

G ee whiz, it's hot. I don't mind hot as much as hot and sticky, which is what it is today. I'd rather be sittin' in the shade with my feet in the brook than out here in the potato patch, 'cept for when it's hot the beetle eggs hatch faster.

Dad docks my allowance a penny for every Colorado potato grub he finds. Ya see, if I can find and squash all eggs before they hatch there won't be any of those red grubs hatching out, which is what eats the potato leaves. You wouldn't believe how fast they grow and how much they can eat. Why I've seen it where there was just stems left. That was before Dad had the idea of hiring me to go after 'em. I can spot the eggs easy enough (they're bright orange) but it sure would be easier if they laid them on top of the leaves. I gotta pull back every plant on both sides to check for the buggers. Once they hatch, the bastards head for the top of the plant to eat where, of course, they are easy for Dad to spot, and he checks the patch pretty regular.

My dad isn't a bad guy. If I do a real good job on the egg clusters, once a week in normal weather and twice a week if it is nasty hot like this, I can kill all of 'em before they hatch. Besides, I can tell when Dad is getting ready to do his tour of the gardens, and I get out there ahead of him just squashing any grubs that I missed. He usually leaves his inspection of the potato rows till last, and I don't think he counts all the ones he sees. I've seen him squash a few without sayin' anything or docking my pay.

I gotta tell ya, this is tedious work, though—bending and looking under the leaves. I try to keep my mind off the heat and the mosquitoes. Mostly I think about Ginny. She's not my girlfriend. I don't even talk to her 'cept maybe saying hi, but she just pops in my mind a lot. She's on my school bus, and I try to work it out so I'm right behind her when we get on the bus coming home, and on a really good day I'll be able to sit behind her—that way, when I'm getting into my seat, I can bend over real close and smell her hair. Gosh, I can almost smell it now. It smells like, gee, I don't know, like the best smelling flower, only better.

She lives on a horse farm nearly five miles away. Last week I rode my bike over to her house…well, to the end of her lane. Her house is down a long lane and all their fields have white fences around them. I was hoping I would see her; maybe she would be out brushing her horse and I could just ride down her lane and say hi. No luck. I just sat there on my bike rocking back and forth wishing I could at least catch a glimpse of her. She has the most wonderful really blond hair.

Outta the potato patch and into the squash and cucumbers. I get paid for picking cucumber beetles. That's the allowance that gets taken out of. Pretty good allowance, I'd say. It only took me two years to save up for my bike. I'm saving up for a car now. I don't get docked for any cucumber beetles Dad finds. They're a lot trickier because you can't see their eggs and when they are grubs (that's before they turn into beetles) they are underground. Worst of all, potato beetles don't hardly ever try to get away, so they're easy to squash, but when cucumber beetles see me they usually stop moving but as soon as I move toward them they fly or drop or run. Ya gotta wonder how they know I'm after 'em and why do they do different things. And how am I going to get down this row without being bored outta my tree?

When I'm not thinking about Ginny, sometimes I get to thinking about the beetles. I've got this game I play with 'em, I pretend they're my friends in another life. Well, it's not exactly another life, I guess it's more like they're up in Heaven lookin' down on me. 'Nother way I look at it is it's like if life was a pinball game, I would be the pinball. But I'd also be playing the pinball game, but as the pinball I wouldn't really know that someone, me, would be playing the game, you know, like Perry thinks his grandfather and God might be watchin' him. Aw, well, I hope you get it. Now in this game it isn't just me and my pinball. In this game I am the star of the show, but my friends can also come into the game as different characters.

So my friends are watching me in the game in the cucumber patch, like they are hanging around the pinball machine, and one of them says, "Let's go play hide and seek with Orvie."

"Count me in! I'm going to freeze when he comes along so he won't see me," says another.

"That won't work. Have you forgotten the yellow stripes on your back? You'd have a better chance if you dropped off the leaf."

"I'm going to do a Peter Pan and fly away," says another one.

Ha, ha, the laugh's on you 'cause you landed on my arm. Squash! I got to admit flying's a pretty good strategy and usually beats me but the one I hate the most is: "I'm going to run down the stem. If he tries to squash me, the spikes on the stem will hurt like hell." Ouch! Now you see, that's not real friendly.

The Worst Day of My Life

Dad an' me are hanging out in the wagon shed, keeping outta the rain. I'm sorting out nuts an' bolts an' washers, of which there are lots that were here when we first moved to the farm when I was five. They're in cans mostly, coffee cans and tobacco cans, lined up on a beam on the wall, and I guess people just put them in the cans to have them handy when they need a bolt for something. Some are rusty and some are greasy, but there aren't any bent ones or ones with messed up threads. I use them whenever I need to. I made a cart out of some scraps of wood and some wheels that came off of something, and the bolts came in handy for doing that, especially the U-bolts, and I had one bolt that went down through the center of the riding board and into the center of the board that I attached the front wheels to with two U-bolts. I put the bolt through a couple of washers between the two boards and I could sit on the riding board with my feet on the steering board and make it go in the direction I wanted. It works pretty good on the road going down the hill to the stone bridge.

Dad's changing the oil in the Jeep. He's always very careful to get the top of the oil can clean before he pushes in the spout. He says dirt is the biggest enemy of an engine. You see, the pistons move up and down in the engine in like a tunnel only really tight and the oil keeps the pistons from rubbing on the tunnels, but if the oil is dirty instead of being smooth it's like sandpaper and it wears out the pistons and then the oil gets into the combustion chamber and burns, and that's why some cars and trucks have a lot of smoke coming out of their exhaust pipes.

When he's done he stands in the door of the wagon shed looking out at the rain and wiping his hands with a rag. It isn't raining very hard but it's kinda chilly so you wouldn't wanna actually do anything outside. I go and stand beside him, and he tells me he's going west and never coming back east. Well, I thought that was OK because out west with the mountains and waterfalls and all looks beautiful in the pictures in my brochures and it sounded exciting when he talked about going west in the Tin Lizzy. But then he says that I'm not coming with him, that I'm to stay with Mom, he says. I ask him why Mom isn't going west and he says he doesn't love her anymore. I look up at him and he just keeps wiping his hands. I don't know what to think. Then Mom comes running out of the house screaming and crying and saying, "Don't! Oh, please don't," and when she sees us she just falls down in the wet grass and sobs. Then I see that I'm crying too. I didn't even notice it. Dad just stands there, and so do I. I don't know what to do. Then Mom gets up and goes back in the house.

I turn my face away so Dad can't see that I'm crying, and I wipe my face with my sleeve. I kinda expect Dad to put his hand on my shoulder or something, but he doesn't. He just stands there. Cubby's there sitting beside me, and I go down and hug him and it feels good.

I stand up and brush off my knees and we stand there some more and then I ask him why I can't go with him, and he says he doesn't love me anymore either, and my eyes start to get wet again so I just kick him and run into the house.

Mom's sitting at the kitchen table with her head resting on her arms. She looks up when she hears the door bang and her eyes and nose are all red and she turns and holds out her arms. I run to her and we hold each other and she keeps saying, "I'm sorry," over and over and hugging me. I'm sorry too, but I'm not sure what I'm sorry about.

Quiet Time

I pretty much just watch Dad when he's around. He gathers up stuff that he'll be able to sell and takes it off to the city when he goes to work. Mostly I don't care, but it makes me sad when he takes the train locomotive that he'd made from plans in a railroad magazine. He had a little metal file cabinet with six drawers and many little compartments where he had really little rivets and pins and screws and different size drill bits that were so small the drill was just like a pencil that would hold a drill bit, and he would turn it with his hand an' make a small hole in the locomotive and then with tweezers he would push in a rivet.

When I was little I got hold of my mother's lipstick and smeared it all over my face. The reason I know this is Dad thought it was so funny he painted a picture of me with the lipstick on. While he was painting me I had to sit real still, and he let me hold a boxcar he had made. I knew that it was fragile and so I stayed very still. He didn't paint the boxcar in my hands but if you saw the picture, you would know that I was holding something special. I wish he hadn't sold it.

When he's home on weekends he works on the Jeep mostly. He made a big box out of aluminum with a hinged top that fits just right on the tailgate of the Jeep. It hangs over the back, and the back canvas of the Jeep fastens to it, which makes the Jeep longer. That's where he will keep his food so animals can't get at it. He made aluminum boxes that fit on both sides of the Jeep hanging out over the back wheels; one of those is for his art brushes and paint and canvases and he puts parts for the Jeep like oil and oil filters and fan belts and soap and tin plates and cups and stuff like that in the other one. He has another piece of aluminum that fills in the space between the back of the seats and the big box. His clothes and things go under that and he has an air mattress and sleeping bag that fill the space from the seat backs to the back of the food box and from side to side, almost a double bed.

He and Mom don't talk much. None of us do, comes right down to it. Dad found a banjo in the attic when he was gathering up things to sell. He had it from before he and Mom got married. For some reason he didn't sell it though. He started playing it and singing one song over and over. I guess it's better than talking.

Dusty Road

Dad left today. Cubby and I watched him check the oil and water in the Jeep, which he did just about every time before he left for anywhere. When he was done he put his hand on my shoulder and said, "Well, son, this is it; I'm on my way. Take care of your mother. Be good." Then he just got in.

The Jeep started right up. It always did. He took good care of it and knew how to fix anything that went wrong. The Jeep turned out of the yard. We watched it go past the barn and the cherry trees. It started to kick up dust till he passed the Webbers' because the road truck puts down oil in front of houses when it gets dry and dusty. After it passed the Webbers' it started to kick up dust again an' then, as it went downhill, it was like it was sinking into the earth until all we could see was the dust. We just stood there watching until we couldn't hear the motor anymore and the dust settled and then we stood there some more. I guess I was thinkin' he would come back. I didn't cry or anything. After a while I got some stones and sat on the bank an' threw 'em across the road at a tree. I'm not a good thrower so I didn't hit the tree very often. Cubby lay down next to me and put his head in my lap.

Then Mom came out of the house and sat down next to me and put her arm around me and we both just sat and then she asked me if I wanted a piece of pie.

168

Blue Cake

The day after he left, my Grandma, Mom's mom, came, which was a good thing because Mom didn't have any money or any way to even go to the store without a car. Grandma had Aunt Hat's car that she inherited when Aunt Hattie died of being too fat. I think Grandma helped Mom out with groceries and loaned her money to buy a car. One of Mom's sisters' husbands was doing pretty well. He worked in the stock market, and I think they helped out some, too.

Mom bought a car. It was a Henry J, a really cheap car, but it was new and it ran good, I mean, ran well. She got a job teaching second grade in my school, well, not exactly my school. I'm in seventh grade which is in a one-room schoolhouse with eighth grade. The two-room schoolhouse where I went used to have all the other grades but it got too crowded and now first grade is in the grange hall and second grade is in a meeting room in the firehouse. Next year all the grades will be in the same building as they are building a big school where they will consolidate all the classes. My class is going to be the first class to graduate from the consolidated school.

It's a good thing they needed teachers because Mom didn't have a proper degree for teaching even though she taught all eight grades at once back before she got married; they told her she could teach as long as she also took classes to get a degree, so she signed up for a night class at Trenton Teachers College.Sometimes I ride to school with her, but I mostly take the bus home rather than hang around and wait for her, because she always has work to do after school lets out. I kinda like being home alone. I can get together with Merry Hand and her five daughters of course—I don't think I'll leave this in if I ever show it to anybody—but mostly I'm hungry when I get home, and whatever I want to eat I have to fix for myself, like peeling carrots or putting cream cheese on celery stalks, and there's always fruit in the house—mostly apples. What I really would like most is a candy bar or cookies, but there isn't anything like that around most times.

Once I made a blue cake. I started off with a recipe in my arithmetic book for muffins. We were learning about fractions. After I had done the recipe it wasn't sweet enough, and also I couldn't find everything I needed. There were some junket tablets and I liked junket when Mom made it so I added some of those. I put in some vanilla and some more sugar and blue food coloring. I was pretty much just putting in anything that was in the cupboard that looked like it might improve my original batter, and then I put it in a cake pan and put it in the oven at the temperature it said in the arithmetic book and set the timer for the time it said. I was thinking Mom would be pretty pleased that I had made dessert.

When the timer went off it wasn't near done. I kept checking it but it didn't rise up like the cakes Mom made. I finally took it out of the oven because I was afraid it might burn. I don't guess I need to tell you that it didn't taste any better than it looked so I guess I'll leave cake making to Mom, which she did that weekend. She made an angel food cake with cherry frosting made with cherries I picked and she put up last summer with my help. That took care of what Mom calls my after school "bottomless pit" for a week.

I was hanging out in the barn when Mom came home. I was about to run out to see if she needed any help with anything, but then I saw that she was crying and didn't go because I thought she probably wanted to be alone.

I worry about her. She was never as fat as Aunt Hat, not even close, but she was pretty well padded all around when Dad left. But now she is skinny, I mean really skinny. Her mom is really skinny, little and skinny. When you saw her next to her sister it was kinda funny because they were about as opposite on the weight scales as you could imagine. Mom used to say, "Soaking wet my mom wouldn't weigh as much as a bag of feed." Mom is taller than Grandma, but I don't think she weighs as much as a bag of feed now. She's going to the doctor about it, but I know it's just 'cause Dad left.

I heard her tell her friends that she feels like a terrible failure, and they tell her it wasn't her fault but she doesn't believe them. I've heard some of them call him names, but Mom asks them not to and she never says anything bad about him, which is good because I'm pretty sure we still love him and, who knows, maybe he'll come back; maybe he'll get tired of painting mountains and waterfalls.

It wasn't bad enough Dad went west to paint and never come east again and what he said, but he sent divorce papers from Reno, Nevada. Mom gets to keep the house, which she hopes she can sell for more than the debt on it.

Move from the Farm

Mom says we're going to move come summer because the house is too big and she can't afford the mortgage payments. She says my uncle who works for the stock market will manage the money she gets for selling the house and we can get by on what she makes teaching. We would have moved last year, but she wanted me to graduate from school with my friends.

We went to look at an apartment today. It's OK, I guess. It's in a house that the owner lives in the other half of. Our door would be on the side by the garage, but we wouldn't be able to use the garage. The door goes right into one room, and there is another room toward the street. The kitchen is toward the back with a bathroom in it. There is just one room upstairs, which also has a bathroom. I don't think much of it, but whatever Mom wants is OK by me.

After looking at the apartment we went to the restaurant just up the street and had cheeseburgers. I had a cherry coke, which is Coca-Cola with cherry syrup (it's really good), and then I had a banana split. Mom said I can have the room upstairs where I'll have my own bathroom, and her bedroom will be the first floor room in the front. I think she's giving me the best deal, but I wasn't going to argue with her. There is a general store, a post office, a Chevy dealer, a church, and a firehouse. It's an easy walk to all those places. I think Mom picked it mostly because it was close to the church and we could walk there on Sundays. When she told me it was a Presbyterian church I was sure that was why she wanted to live there.

She got me to join the Presbyterian Church soon after Dad left. I had to go once a week to the preacher's house, which was right across the street from his church, that big church with the organ pipes and the stained-glass windows. We sat in his parlor, and he taught me about the Bible. He was a funny little guy, not as tall as I am, and he was mostly bald with a fringe of hair around his head just above his ears. He was nice though and I pretty much liked him. He mostly taught me about Jesus and the parables he told, which I thought were pretty good lessons.

On Sundays Mom went to church and I had to go to Sunday school. I didn't care for it much, but I learned more Bible stories. I didn't believe all of them, like Moses making the water of the Red Sea part so his people could walk across and Daniel not getting eaten by lions. And then came the Sunday I was accepted into the church and was called down to the front with some other people. After that I was a Presbyterian. I guess that's a permanent thing because Mom said she had joined when she was a little girl and she was still a Presbyterian even though she hadn't gone to church for a lot of years.

I wonder if Dad misses me. When I graduate from high school I'm going out West and see if I can get him and Mom back together.

Cubby and I Take a Walk

"Mom, I'm going up the hill."

"OK, Orvie. We'll be eating in about an hour."

This spring the stream is about as high as it ever gets, flowing around the rock I put in it to make a dam. The dam washed out pretty soon after I made it, but the rock is still there. Cubby and I walk along the stream to where it flows into the brook, and then we head along the bank of the brook until we come to the limb that I used to get across to the other side. Cubby jumps into the water as usual and takes a big drink. I've trained him to face me when he shakes the water off so he doesn't get me wet. The deer path through the thicket is pretty muddy, and I have to find roots and hummocks to step on to keep from getting mud in my sneakers. At the top of the hill we go through the woods to the farm road to check out the back of our property. I kinda smile, remembering the time Dad was riding Bessie down this road and thought he was showing her who was boss when she turned and he went straight. I can see some of the sticks where I made a fort when I was little.

I come back to the edge of the woods and sit with my back against a tree. Cubby and I can see the whole farm from here: the old apple orchard (the new ones Dad had planted never got going, what with Bessie getting loose and scratching her belly on those little trees and the goats getting loose and eating them), the garden, which is a tangled mess of weeds now, and the hay field in back of the house out to the hedge row that's our other property line, and the two big old cherry trees almost as tall as the barn.

I scratch Cubby between the ears. "'Member when I used to spit cherry pits at you from up in the tree?"

Bessie's gone now. Jessie, the man who sold her to us, came and got her. I don't think he paid Dad anything for her. She probably went to the glue factory. Dad sold the goats and got rid of the chickens. We get eggs from Rudy now. We haven't had pigs for several years, so it's pretty quiet around here.

"Mom and I are leaving and we can't take you with us." Cubby and I just sit there looking out over the farm. There won't be much of a sunset today, as there are dark clouds out to the west.

"You met the people who are buying the farm. They seem like nice folks, and they said they would keep you."

I turn and he is looking at me. "I'm sorry." I think he knows the word "sorry," but I don't think he knows why I'm sorry.

"We're going to live on a busy highway where cars and trucks go really fast. I'd be worried that you'd be hit. You wouldn't like it there. There are no fields for you to run in. We'd have to keep you chained up."

He licks my face. "You know I'll always love you." I push my face into his neck and hug him.

I get up and start down the hill. My steps get longer as gravity pulls me until I am almost running.